William Hayley, John Aikin

A View of the Life, Travels and Philanthropic Labors of the late John Howard

William Hayley, John Aikin

A View of the Life, Travels and Philanthropic Labors of the late John Howard

ISBN/EAN: 9783337346157

Printed in Europe, USA, Canada, Australia, Japan

Cover: Foto ©Raphael Reischuk / pixelio.de

More available books at **www.hansebooks.com**

A VIEW,

OF THE

LIFE, TRAVELS,

AND

PHILANTHROPIC LABORS

OF THE LATE

JOHN HOWARD,

ESQUIRE, L. L. D. F. R. S.

By JOHN AIKIN, M. D.

*In Commune auxilium natus, ac publicum bonum,
ex quo dabit cuique partem: etiam ad calamitosos,
pro portione, improbandos et emendandos, bonitatem
suam permittet.* SENECA.

PHILADELPHIA:

PRINTED FOR JOHN ORMROD, BY W. W. WOODWARD,

At Franklin's Head, No. 41, Chesnut-street.

1794.

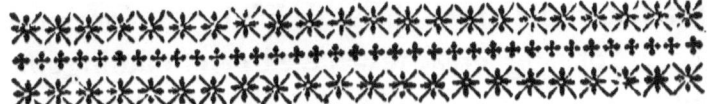

INTRODUCTION.

IF it be a juſt obſervation, that every man
who has attained uncommon eminence in
his particular line of purſuit, becomes an object
worthy of the public notice, how forcibly muſt ſuch
a maxim apply to that ſpecies of excellence which
renders a man the greateſt benefactor to his fellow-creatures, and the nobleſt ſubject of their contemplation ? Beneficence, pure in its intentions,
wiſe and comprehenſive in its plans, and active
and ſuccefsful in execution, muſt ever ſtand at
the head of thoſe qualities which elevate the human character ; and mankind cannot have a concern ſo important, as the diffuſion of ſuch a ſpirit, by means of the moſt perfect and impreſſive
examples, in which it has actually been diſplayed.

Among thoſe truly illuſtrious perſons who, in
the ſeveral ages and nations of the world, have

marked their track through life by a continued course of *doing good*, few have been so distinguished, either by the extent of the good produced, or the purity of motive and energy of character exhibited in the process of doing it, as the late Mr. HOWARD. To have adopted the cause of the prisoner, the sick, and the destitute, not only in his own country, but throughout all Europe ; to have considerably alleviated the burden of present misery among those unfortunate classes, and at the same time to have provided for the reformation of the vicious, and the prevention of future crimes and calamities ;—to have been instrumental in the actual establishment of many plans of humanity and utility, and to have laid the foundation for much more improvement hereafter ;—and to have done all this as a private unaided individual, struggling with toils, dangers and difficulties, which might have appalled the most resolute ; is surely a range of beneficence which scarcely ever before came within the compass of one man's exertions. Justly, then, does the name of *Howard* stand among those which confer the highest honor on the English character ; and, since his actions cannot fail to transmit his memory with glory to posterity, it is incumbent on his countrymen and cotemporaries, for

their own fakes, to tranfmit correfponding me-
morials of their veneration and gratitude.

It would, indeed, be a convincing proof of the
increafed good fenfe and virtue of the age, if
fuch characters as this were found to rife in the
comparative fcale of fame and applaufe. Long e-
nough have mankind weakly paid their admiration
as the reward of pernicious exertions,—of talents,
often very moderate in themfelves, and only rendered confpicuous by the blaze of mifchief they
have kindled. It is now furely time that men
fhould know and diftinguifh their benefactors
from their foes ; and that the nobleft incitements
to action fhould be given to thofe actions only
which are directed to the general welfare.

Since the lamented death of this excellent perfon, there have not been wanting refpectable eu-
logies of his character, and fuch biographical notices concerning him, as might in fome meafure
gratify that public curiofity which is awakened
by every celebrated name. There is yet wanting, however, what I confider as by much the
moft valuable tribute to the memory of every
man diftinguifhed by public fervices ; I mean a
portraiture of him, modelled upon thofe circumftances which rendered him eminent ; difplaying

in their rise and progress those features of character which so peculiarly fitted him for the part he undertook, the origin and gradual developement of his great designs, and all the successive steps by which they were brought to their final state of maturity. It is this branch of biographical writing that alone entitles it to rank high among the compositions relative to human life and manners. Nature, indeed, has implanted in us a desire of becoming acquainted with those circumstances belonging to a distinguished character which are common to him and the mass of mankind ; and it is therefore right that such a desire should in some degree be gratified : but to make *that* the principal object of attention, which, but for its association with somewhat more important, would not at all deserve notice, is surely to reverse the value of things, and to estimate the mass by the quantity of its alloy, rather than by that of the precious metal.

The deficiency which I have stated relative to Mr. *Howard*, it is my present object, as far as I am able, to supply ; and however the task in some respect may be beyond my powers, yet the advantage I enjoyed of a long and confidential intercourse with him during the publication of his works, and of frequent conversation with him concerning the paſt and future objects of his enquiries, together with the communications with which I have been favoured by ſome of his moſt intimate friends,—will, I hope, juſtify me in the eye of the public for taking it on my-ſelf. I truſt I have already appeared not infen-ſible to his exalted merit, nor indifferent to his reputation.

One thing more I think it neceſſary to ſay concerning this attempt. It has been more than once ſuggeſted in print, but, I believe, without any foundation, that a life of Mr. *Howard* might be expected to appear under the ſanction and au-thority of his *family*. It is proper for me to avow, that this is not *that* work. The undertaking is perfectly ſpontaneous on my part, without encou-ragement from his relations or repreſentatives. Mr. *Howard* was a man with whom every one capable of feeling the excellence and dignity of his character, might claim kindred ; and *they* were the neareſt to him whom he made the con-fidents and depoſitaries of his deſigns.

A VIEW

OF THE

LIFE, TRAVELS, AND PHILANTHROPIC LABORS

OF THE LATE

John Howard, Efq. L.L.D.F.R.S.

JOHN HOWARD was born, according to the beſt information I am able to obtain, about the year 1727. His father was an up-holſterer and carpet-warehouſe man in Long-lane, Smithfield, who, having acquired a hand-ſome fortune retired from buſineſs, and had a houſe firſt at Enfield, and afterwards at Hack-ney. It was, I believe, at the former of theſe places that Mr. *Howard* was born.

As Mr. *Howard*'s father was a ſtrict Proteſt-ant diſſenter, it was natural for him to educate his ſon under a preceptor of the ſame principles. But his choice for this purpofe was the fource of a lafting misfortune, which, as it has been too frequent an occurrence, deferves particular notice. There was at that time a fchoolmafter at fome diftance from London, who, in confequence of his moral and religious character, had been intrufted with the education of the children of moft of the opulent diffenters in the metropolis, though extremely deficient in the qualifications requifite for fuch an office*. That perfons whofe own education and habits of life have rendered them very inadequate judges of the talents neceffary for an inftructor of youth, fhould eafily fall into this error, is not to be wondered at : but the evil is a real one, though its caufe be excufeable : and, as fmall communities with ftrong party attachments are peculiarly liable to this mifplaced confidence, it is right that they fhould in a particular manner be put on their

---

* I find it afferted in fome memoirs of Mr. *Howard* in the *Univerfal Magazine,* that this perfon (whofe name is there mentioned) was a man of confiderable learning, and author of a tranflation of the New Teftament and of a Latin grammar. Without enquiring how far this may fet afide the charge of his be ng deficient as an inftructor, I think it proper to fay, that my only foundation for that charge is Mr. *Howard's* own authority.

guard againſt it. They who know the diſſenters, will acknowledge, that none appear more ſenſible of the importance of a good education, or leſs ſparing in their endeavours to procure it for their children ; nor, upon the whole, can it be ſaid that they are unſucceſsful in their attempts. Indeed, the very confined ſyſtem of inſtruction adopted in the public ſchools of this kingdom, renders it no difficult taſk to vie with them in the attainment of objects of real utility. But if it be made a leading purpoſe to train up youth in a certain ſet of opinions, and for this end it be thought eſſential that the maſter ſhould be excluſively choſen from among thoſe who are the moſt cloſely attached to them, it is obvious that a ſmall community muſt lie under great comparative diſadvantages.

The event with reſpect to Mr. *Howard*, was, (as he aſſured me, with greater indignation than I have heard him expreſs upon many ſubjects), that, after a continuance of ſeven years at this ſchool, he left it, not fully taught any one thing. The loſs of this period was irreparable ; he felt it all his life after, and it was but too obvious to thoſe who converſed with him. From this ſchool he was removed to Mr. Eames' academy ; but his continuance there muſt, I con-

ceive, have been of fhort duration ; and, whatever might be his acquifitions in that place,
he certainly did not fupply the deficiencies of
his earlier education. As fome of the accounts
publifhed concerning him, might inculcate the
idea that he had attained confiderable proficiency in letters, I feel myfelf obliged, from my own
knowledge, to affert, that he was never able to
fpeak or write his native language with gram-
matical correctnefs, and that his acquaintance
with other languages (the French, perhaps, ex-
cepted) was flight and fuperficial. In eftimating
the powers of his mind, it rather adds to the account, that he had this additional difficulty to
combat in his purfuit of the great objects of his
later years. ·

Mr. *Howard*'s father died when he was
young, and bequeathed to him and a daughter,
his only children, confiderable fortunes. He directed in his will, that his fon fhould not come
to the poffeffion of his property till his twenty-
fifth year.

It was, probably, in confequence of the father's
direction that he was bound apprentice to a
wholefale grocer in the city. This will appear
a fingular ftep in the education of a young man

of fortune ; but, at that period, inuring youth to habits of method and induſtry, and giving them a prudent regard to money, with a knowledge of the modes of employing it to advantage, were by many confidered as the moſt important points in every condition of life. Mr. *Howard* was probably indebted to this part of his education for fome of that fpirit of order, and knowledge of common affairs, which he poſſeſſed ; but he did not in this fituation contract any of that love of aggrandifement which is the bafis of all commercial exertions ; and fo irkſome was the employment to him, that, on coming of age, he bought out the remainder of his time, and immediately fet out on his travels to France and Italy.

On his return he mixed with the world, and lived in the ſtyle of other young men of leifure and fortune. He had acquired that taſte for the arts which the view of the moſt perfect examples of them is fitted to create ; and, notwithſtanding the defects of his education, he was not without an attachment to reading and the ſtudy of nature. The delicacy of his conſtitution, however, induced him to take lodgings in the country, where for fome time his health was the principal object of his attention. As he was fuppofed to be of a confumptive habit, he was put upon a rigorous regimen of diet, which laid the foundation of that extraordinary abftemioufnefs and indifference to the gratifications of the palate which ever after fo much diftinguifhed him. It is probable that, from his firft appearance in a ftate of independence, his way of thinking and acting was marked by a certain fingularity. Of this, one of the moft remarkable confequences was his firft marriage about his twenty-fifth year. As a return of gratitude to Mrs. *Sarah Lardeau* (or *Loidore*), widow, with whom he lodged at Stoke Newington, for her kind attention to him during his invalid ftate, he propofed marriage to her, though fhe was twice his age, and extremely fickly; and, notwithftanding her remonftrances on the impropriety of fuch an union, he perfifted in his defign, and it took place. She is reprefented as a fenfible, worthy woman; and on her death, three years afterwards (during which interval he continued at Newington), Mr. *Howard* was fincerely affected with his lofs; nor did he ever fail to mention her with refpect, after his fentiments of things may have been fuppofed, from greater commerce with the world, to have undergone a change.

His liberality with refpect to pecuniary concerns was early difplayed ; and at no time of
his life does he feem to have confidered money
in any other light than as an inftrument of procuring happinefs to himfelf and others. The
little fortune that his wife poffeffed he gave to
her fifter ; and during his refidence at Newington he beftowed much in charity, and made
a handfome donation to the diffenting congregation there, for the purpofe of providing a
dwelling-houfe for the minifter.

His attachment to religion was a principle
imbibed from his earlieft years, which continued fteady and uniform through life. The body
of Chriftians to whom he particularly united
himfelf were the Independents, and his fyftem
of belief was that of the moderate Calvinifts.
But though he feems early to have made up his
mind as to the doctrines he thought beft founded, and the mode of worfhip he moft approved,
yet religion abftractedly confidered, as the relation between man and his Maker, and the
grand fupportof morality, appears to have been
the principal object of his regard. He was lefs
folicitous about modes and opinions, than the
internal fpirit of piety and devotion ; and in
his eltimate of different religious focieties, the

circumstances to which he principally attended, were their zeal and sincerity. As it is the nature of sects in general, to exhibit more earnestness in doctrine, and strictness in discipline, than the establishment from which they dissent, it is not to be wondered at that a person of Mr. *Howard's* disposition should regard the various denominations of sectaries with predilection, and attach himself to their most distinguished members. In London he seems chiefly to have joined the Baptist congregation in Wild-street, long under the ministry of the much-respected Dr. Stennett. His connexions were, I believe, least with that class called the Rational Dissenters; yet he probably had not a more intimate friend in the world than Dr. Price, who always ranked among them. It was his constant practice to join in the service of the establishment when he had not the opportunity of attending a place of dissenting worship; and though he was warmly attached to the interests of the party he espoused, yet he had that true spirit of catholicism, which led him to honour virtue and religion wherever he found them, and to regard the *means* only as they were subservient to the *end.*

He was created a Fellow of the Royal Society on May 13, 1756. This honour was not,

I prefume, conferred upon him in confequence of any extraordinary proficiency in fcience which he had manifefted ; but rather in conformity to the laudable practice of that fociety, of attaching gentlemen of fortune and leifure to the interefts of knowledge, by incorporating them into their body. Mr. *Howard* was not unmindful of the obligation he lay under to contribute fomething to the common ftock of information. Three fhort papers of his are publifhed in the *Tranfactions.* Thefe are,.

In Vol. LIV. On the Degree of Cold obferved at Card ngton in the Winter of 1763; when Bird's Thermometer was as low as 10; .

In Vol. LVII. On the Heat of the Waters at Bath, containing a Table of the Heat of the Waters of the different Baths.

In Vol. LXI. On the Heat of the Ground on Mount Vefuvius.

This lift may ferve to give an idea of the kind and degree of his philofophical refearch. Meteorological obfervations were much to his tafte ; and even in his later tours, when he was occupied by very different objects, he never

travelled without fome inftruments for that
purpofe. I have heard him likewife mention
fome experiments on the effects of the union of
the primary colours in different proportions, in
which he employed himfelf with fome affiduity.

After the death of his wife, in the year 1756,
he fet out upon another tour, intending to commence it with a vifit to the ruins of Lifbon.
The event of this defign will be hereafter mentioned. He remained abroad a few months;
and, on his return, began to alter the houfe on
his eftate at Cardington near Bedford, where
he fettled. In 1758 he made a very fuitable
alliance with Mifs *Henrietta Leeds*, eldeft
daughter of Edward Leeds, Efq. of Croxton,
Cambridgefhire, king's ferjeant ; and fifter of
the prefent Edward Leeds, Efq. a Mafter in
Chancery, and of Jofeph Leeds, Efq. of Croy-
don. With this lady, who poffeffed in an eminent degree all the mild and amiable virtues
proper to her fex, he paffed, as I have often
heard him declare, the only years of true enjoyment which he had known in life. Soon after his marriage he purchafed Watcombe, in
the New Foreft, Hampfhire, and removed thi-

ther. Concerning his way of life in this pleasant retreat, I find nothing characteristic to relate, except the state of perfect security and harmony in which he managed to live in the midst of a people, against whom his predecessor thought it necessary to employ all the contrivances of engines and guns in order to preserve himself from their hostilities. He had, indeed, none of those propensities which so frequently embroil country gentlemen with their neighbours, both small and great. He was no sportsman, no executor of the game laws, and in no respect an encroacher on the rights and advantages of others. In possessing him, the poor could not fail soon to find that they had acquired a protector and benefactor; and I am unwilling to believe that in any part of the world these relations are not returned with gratitude and attachment. After continuing at Watcombe three or four years, he sold the place, and went back to Cardington, which thenceforth became his fixed residence.

Here he steadily pursued those plans, both with respect to the regulation of his personal and family concerns and to the promotion of the good of those around him, which principle and inclination led him to approve. Though without the ambition of making a fplendid appearance, he had a tafte for elegant neatnefs in his habitation and furniture. His fobriety of manners and peculiarities of living did not fit him for much promifcuous fociety; yet no man received his felect friends with more true hofpitality; and he always maintained an intercourfe with feveral of the firft perfons in his county, who knew and refpected his worth. Indeed, however uncomplying he might be with the freedoms and irregularities of polite life, he was by no means negligent of its received forms; and, though he might be denominated a man of fcruples and fingularities, no one would difpute his claim to the title of a gentleman.

But the terms on which he held fociety with perfons of his own condition, are of much lefs importance in the view I mean to take of his character, than the methods by which he rendered himfelf a blefling to the indigent and friendlefs in a fmall circle, before he extended his benevolence to fo wide a compafs. It feems to have been the capital object of his ambition, that the poor in his village fhould be the moft orderly in their manners, the neateft in their perfons and habitations, and poffeffed of the

greateſt ſhare of the comforts of life, that could
be met with in any part of England. And as
it was his diſpoſition to carry every thing he
undertook to the greateſt pitch of perfection,
ſo he ſpared no pains or expence to effect this
purpoſe. He began by building a number of
neat cottages on his eſtate, annexing to each a
little land for a garden, and other conveniencies. In this project, which might be conſidered as an object of taſte as well as of benevolence, he had the full concurrence of his excellent partner. I remember his relating,
that once, having ſettled his accounts at the
cloſe of a year, and found a balance in his favor, he propoſed to his wife to make uſe of it
in a journey to London, or any other gratification ſhe choſe. " What a pretty cottage
it would build," was her anſwer ; and the money was ſo employed. Theſe comfortable habitations he peopled with the moſt induſtrious
and ſober tenants he could find ; and over them
he exerciſed the ſuperintendence of maſter and
father combined. He was careful to furniſh
them with employment, to aſſiſt them in ſick-
neſs and diſtreſs, and to educate their children.
In order to preſerve their morals, he made it
a condition that they ſhould regularly attend
their ſeveral places of worſhip, and abſtain

from public houfes, and from fuch amufements as he though: pernicious; and he fecured their compliance with his rules by making them te-nants at will.

I fhall here beg leave to digrefs a little, in order to make fome general obfervations on the different methods that may be propofed for bettering the condition of the loweft and moft numerous clafs among us. In the ftate in which they too frequently appear, depreffed to the extremeft point of indigence, unable by their utmoft exertions to obtain more than the bare neceffaries of exiftence, debafed by the total want of inftruction, and partaking of nothing that can dignify the human character, it is no wonder that a benevolent perfon of the higher ranks in fociety fhould confider them as crea-tures of an inferior fpecies, only to be benefit-ed by the conftant exercife of his authority and fuperintendence. And I believe the fact to be, that, from the operation of our poor laws, and other circumftances, the poor in this country are more thoughtlefs, improvident, and helplefs, than thofe of almoft any other na-tion. Humanity will, therefore, in fuch a ftate of things, think it neceffary to affume the entire management of thofe who can neither think nor act for their own good ; and will direct and over-rule all their concerns, juft as it would thofe of children and idiots. In fhort, it will aim at fuch a kind of influence, as the Jefuits of Paraguay eftablifhed, (perhaps with the fame benevolent views) over the fimple natives.

But is this ftate of pupilage to be perpetual ? and, in a land of liberty and equal laws, is the great body of people always to exift in a condtion of actual fubjection to and dependence on the few ? Are they never to be intrufted with their own happinefs, but always to look up for fuppoit and direction to thofe who in reality are lefs independent than themfelves ? This is an idea which a liberal mind will be unwilling to admit ; and it will anxioufly look forward to a period, in which meannefs of condition fhall not neceffarily imply debafement of nature ; but thofe of EVERY rank in fociety, feeling powers within themfelves to fecure their effential comforts, fhall rely upon their own exertions, and be guided by the dictates of their own reafon. That this is not an imaginary ftate of things the general condition of the lowest classes in some countries, and even in some parts of England where the working poor, at the same time that their earnings enable them to procure the comforts of life, are inured to habits of sobriety and frugality, is a sufficient proof.

There are few counties in England which afford less employment to a numerous poor than that of Bedford ; of course, wages are low, and much distress would prevail, were it not for the humanity of the gentlemen who reside upon their estates. Among these Mr. Howard distinguished himself by a peculiar attention to the comfort and improvement of his dependents ; and he was accordingly held by them in the highest respect and veneration. I may add, that he possessed their LOVE ; which is not always the case with those who render essential services to the people of that class. But he treated them with kindness, as well as beneficence ; and he particularly avoided every thing stern or imperious in his manner towards them. Whatever there might appear of strictness in the discipline he enforced, it had only in view their best interests ; and if under his protection they could pass a tranquil old age in their own comfortable cottages, rather than

end their lives in a work-houfe, the fubordination to which they fubmitted was amply com-
penfated. It is certain that the melioration of
manners and principles which he promoted,
was the moft effectual means of eventually rendering them more independent; and I have
reafon to know, that, latterly at leaft, he was
as well affected to the rights, as he was folicitous to augment the comforts of the poor.

His charities were not confined to thofe more
immediately connected with his property;
they took in the whole circle of neighbourhood. His bounty was particularly directed to
that fundamental point in improving the condition of the poor, giving them a fober and
ufeful education. From early life he attended to this object; and he eftablifhed fchools for
both fexes, conducted upon the moft judicious
plan. The girls were taught reading, and
needle-work in a plain way: the boys reading,
and fome of them writing, and the rudiments
of arithmetic. They were regularly to attend
public worfhip in the way their parents approved. The number brought up in thefe fchools
was fluctuating, but the inftitutions were unin-
terrupted. In every other way in which a
man thoroughly difpofed to do good with the
means Providence has beftowed upon him, can

C

exercife his liberality, Mr. Howard ftood among the foremoft. He was not only a fub-fcriber to various public fchemes of benevo-lence, but his private charities were largely diffufed, and remarkably well directed. It was, indeed, only to his particular confidents and coadjutors that many of thefe were ever knawn; but they render him the moft ample teftimony in this refpect. His very intimate and confidential friend, the Rev. Mr. Tho-mas Smith of Bedford, gives me the following account of this part of his conduct, at a time when he was deeply engaged in thofe public exertions which might be fuppofed to interfere with his private and local benefactions. "He ftill continued to devife liberal things for his poor neighbours and tenants; and, confider-ing how much his heart and time were engag-ed in his great and comprehenfive plans, it was furprifing with what minutenefs he would fend home his directions about his private do-nations. His fchools were continued to the laft." It is impoffible any ftronger proof can be given, that the habit of doing good was wrought into his very nature, than that, while his public actions placed him without a rival for deeds of philanthropy, he fhould ftill be un-able to fatisfy his benevolent defires without his accuſtomed benefits to his neighbours and dependents.

Another early feature of that character which Mr. Howard afterwards ſo conſpicuouſly diſplayed, was a determined reſiſtance of injuſtice and oppreſſion. No one could be more firmly relied on as the protector of right and innocence againſt unfeeling and unprincipled power. His indignation was rouſed by any attempts to encroach or domineer; and his ſpirit led him, without heſitation, to expreſs, both in words and actions, his ſenſe of ſuch conduct. As no man could be more perfectly independent, both in mind and ſituation, than himſelf, he made that uſe of his advantage which every independent man ought to do;—he acted as principle directed him, regardleſs whom he might diſpleaſe by it; he ſtrongly marked his different ſenſations with reſpect to different characters; and he was not leſs ſtrenuous in oppoſing pernicious ſchemes, than in promoting beneficial ones.

The love of order and regularity likewiſe marked the early as well as the later periods of his life; it directed his own domeſtic concerns equally with his plans for the benefit of others. His difpofition of time was exact and methodical. He accurately knew the ftate of all his affairs; and the hand of economy regulated what the heart of generofity difpenfed. His tafte in drefs, furniture, and every thing exterior, was turned to fimplicity and neatnefs; and this conformity of difpofition rendered him an admirer of the fect of Quakers, with many individuals of which he maintained an intimate connection.

In common with many other benevolent and virtuous characters, he had a fondnefs for gardening, and the cultivation of plants both ufeful and ornamental. Indeed, as his own diet was almoft entirely of the vegetable kind, he had various inducements to attend to this pleafing occupation. That moft valuable root, the potatoe, was a great favourite with him; and a remarkably productive fpecies of it, which he recommended to public notice, was diftinguifhed by his name. His garden was an object of curiofity, both for the elegant manner in which it was laid out, and for the excellence of its productions; and in his various travels he frequently brought home, and diftributed among his friends, the feeds of curious kinds of cultivated vegetables.

In this manner Mr. Howard paffed the tranquil years of his fettled refidence at Cardington; happy in himfelf, and the inftrument of good to all around him. But this ftate was not long to continue. His domeftic felicity received a fatal wound from the death of his beloved wife, in the year 1765, foon after delivery of her only child. It is unneceffary to fay how a heart like his muft have felt on fuch an event. They who have been witneffes of the fenfibility with which, many years afterwards, he recollected it, and know how he honored and cherifhed her memory, will conceive his fenfations at that trying period. He was thenceforth attached to his home only by the duties annexed to it; of which the moft interefting was the education of his infant fon. This was an office which almoft immediately commenced; for according to his ideas, education had place from the very firft dawn of the mental faculties. The very unfortunate iffue of his cares, with refpect to his fon, has caufed a charge to be brought againft him very deeply affecting his paternal character. That this charge was in its main circumftance falfe and calumnious, has, I truft, been proved, to the fatisfaction of the public, by appeals to facts which have remained uncontroverted. I fhall not, therefore, go over again the ground of this controverfy; but fhall rather follow the proper line of this work, by briefly difplaying Mr. Howard's ideas on education, and his manner of executing them.

Regarding children as creatures poffeffed of ftrong paffions and defires, without reafon and experience to controul them, he thought that nature feemed, as it were, to mark them out as the fubjects of abfolute authority; and that the firft and fundamental principle to be inculcated upon them, was implicit and unlimited obedience. This cannot be effected by any procefs of reafoning, before reafon has its commencement; and therefore muft be the refult of coercion. Now, as no man ever more effectually combined the *leniter in modo* with the *fortiter in re,* the coercion he practifed was calm and gentle, but at the fame time fteady and refolute. I fhall give an inftance of it which I had from himfelf. His child one day, wanting fomething which he was not to have, fell into a fit of crying, which the nurfe could not pacify. Mr. Howard took him from her, and laid him quietly in his lap, till, fatigued with crying, he became ftill. This procefs, a few times repeated, had fuch an effect, that the child, if crying ever fo violently, was rendered quiet the inftant his father took him. In a fimilar manner, without harfh words and threats, ftill lefs blows, he gained every other point which he thought neceffary to gain, and brought the child to fuch a habit of obedience, that I have heard him fay, he believed his fon would have put his finger into the fire if he had commanded him. Certain it is, that many fathers could not, if they approved it, execute a plan of this kind; but Mr. Howard in this cafe cnly purfued the general method which he took to effect any thing which a thorough conviction of its propriety induced him to undertake. It is abfurd, therefore, to reprefent him as wanting that milk of human kindnefs for his only fon, with which he abounded for the reft of his fellow-creatures; for he aimed at what he thought the good of both, by the very fame means; and, if he carried the point further with refpect to his fon, it was only becaufe he was more interefted in his welfare. But this courfe of difcipline, whatever be thought of it, could not have been long practifed, fince the child was early fent to fchool, and the father lived very little at home afterwards. As to its effect en the youth's mind (if that, and not intention, be the circumftance on which Mr.

Howard's vindication is to depend), I confider
it as a manifeft impoffibility, that controuling
the child, fhould have been the caufe of the
young man's infanity. If any fuch remote
caufe could be fuppofed capable of producing
fuch an effect, the oppofite extreme of indulgence would have been a much more likely one.
But I think it highly probable, that a father,
whofe prefence was affociated with the per-
ception of reftraint and refufal, fhould always
have infpired more awe than affection ; and
fhould never have created that filial confidence,
which is both the moft pleafing and moft falutary of the fentiments attending that relation.
And this has been the great evil of that rigorous mode of education, once fo general, and
ftill frequent, among perfons of a particular
perfuafion. I have authority to fay, that Mr.
Howard was at length fenfible that he had in
fome meafure miftaken the mode of forming his
fon to that character he wifhed him to acquire ;
though, with refpect to his mental derangement, I know that he imputed no blame to
himfelf on that head. With what parental
forrow he was affected by that event will appear in the progrefs of the narration.

Having now given such a view of the temper and manners of this excellent person, in his private situation, as may serve to introduce him to the reader's acquaintance at the time of his assuming a public character, I shall, without further delay, proceed to trace him through those years of his life, the employment of which alone has rendered him an object of the curiosity and admiration of his countrymen.

In the year 1773, Mr. Howard was nominated High-Sheriff of the county of Bedford. An obstacle, however, lay in the way of his accepting that office, concerning which I shall take the liberty of making a few remarks.

When a principled Dissenter, whose condition in life permits him to aspire to the honor of serving his country in some post of magistracy, reflects on his situation, he finds that he must make his election of one of the three following determinations. He must either comply with a religious rite of another church, merely on account of its being made the condition of receiving the office ; or take upon himself the office without such compliance, under all the hazard that attends it ; or he must quietly sit down under that vacation from public charges which the ftate, in its wifdom, has impofed upon him, fatisfied with promoting the welfare of individuals by modes not interdicted to him. It would be great prefumption in me to decide which of thefe determinations is moft conformable to duty. In fact, there is only a choice of difficulties, and the decifion between them muft be left to every man's own feelings, which, if his intentions be good and honeft, will fcarcely lead him wrong. But it was perfectly fuitable to Mr. Howard's character to make option of the office with the hazard: for as, on the one hand, no confideration on earth could have induced him to violate his religious principles; fo, on the other, his active difpofition, and zeal for the public good, ftrongly impelled him to affume a ftation, in which thofe qualities might have free fcope for exertion; and as to perfonal hazard, that was never an obftacle in his way. There may be cafuifts who will condemn this choice, and regard it as a ferious offence againft the laws of his country, to have taken upon him an office without complying with its preliminary conditions. But, I conceive, the fincere philanthropift will rather make a different reflection, and feel a fhock in thinking, that, had Mr. Howard been influenced by thofe apprehenfions which would have operated upon moſt men, he would have been excluded from that ſituation, which gave occaſion to all thoſe ſervices which he rendered to humanity in his own country, and throughout Europe*.

He entered upon his office with the reſolution of performing all its dutics with that punctuality which marked his conduct in every thing he undertook. Of theſe, one of the moſt important, though leaſt agreeable, is the inſpection of the PRISONS within its juriſdiction. But this, to him, was not only an act of duty, it intereſted him as a material concern of humanity.

* *The penalties to which Mr. Howard, in this inſtance, expoſed himſelf, are declared in the following clauſe of the* Teſt Act, *which cannot too often be placed before the eyes of Britons.* " Every perſon that ſhall
" neglect or refuſe to take the ſacrament as aforeſaid,
" and yet, after ſuch neglect or refuſal, ſhall execute
" any of the ſaid offices or employments, and being
" thereupon lawfully convicted, ſhall be diſabled to
" ſue, or uſe any action, bill, plaint or information,
" in courſe of law, or to proſecute any ſuit in any
" court of equity, or to be guardian of any child,
" or executor or adminiſtrator of any perſon, or

The attention of Mr. Howard to perſons
"ſick and in priſon," is by himſelf dated as far
back as the year 1756, when he was induced by
a ſingular, but what I ſhould call a ſublime, curioſity to viſit Liſbon, then lying in the recent
ruins of its terrible earthquake.   The packet

" capable of any legacy or deed of gift, or to bear
" any office ; and ſhall forfeit the ſum of five hun-
" dred pounds, to be recovered by him or them
" that ſhall ſue for the ſame."—*In the debate on the
repeal of this act, the mover, with much eloquence, introduced the very caſe of Mr. Howard, and ſeemed con-
ſiderably to impreſs his audience by the ſuppoſition of
ſuch a man ſuffering its penalties, in conſequence of
an information which any villain might lay againſt
him.   In reply it was ſaid, that, whatever were a
man's intentions, if he voluntarily contravened a known
law of his country, it ought not to be reckoned a hard-
ſhip that he incurred the penalties by which it was
ſanctioned.   And this reaſoning is undoubtedly juſt, as
it reſpects the intereſt of an individual put in competi-
tion with the ſecurity of a law.   But ſurely it is a
proper. conſideration for the legiſlature, whether a
law be grounded on thoſe principles of equity and general utility which can juſtify the impoſition of ſuch
dreadful penalties for the breach of it, eſpecially when
experience has ſhewn, that the moſt conſcientious and
well-intentioned perſons are moſt liable to incur them.*

in which he failed being taken by a French privateer, he, with the rest of the crew, was first exposed to all the barbarities exercised by those licensed pirates, who possess the right of the sword, not molified by the feelings of gentlemen; and, on his arrival in France, he for a time endured some of the hardships of a prisoner of war, and became acquainted with all the sufferings of his countrymen in the same situation. These, on his return to England, he took care to make known to the Commissioners of Sick and Wounded Seamen, who gave him their thanks for his information, and exerted themselves to obtain redress. It was impossible that so feeling a lesson of the calamities inflicted upon the unprotected classes of mankind, by fellow-creatures " dressed in a little brief authority," should fail to make a durable impression on such a mind as Mr. Howard's.

It was not, however, till the period of his serving the office of sheriff, that the distresses of those confined in the civil prisons of his own country engaged his particular notice. In the introduction to his *State of the Prisons,* he has with the most unassuming simplicity, related the gradual progress of his enquiries; and in

D

what manner he was led, from an examination of the gaols in his own fmall county, to an inveftigation of all the circumftances belonging to this branch of police throughout the kingdom.

The firft thing which ftruck him, was the enormous injuftice of remanding to prifon for the payment of FEES, thofe who had been acquitted or difcharged without trial. As the magiftrates of his county, though willing to redrefs this grievance, did not conceive themfelves poffeffed of the power of granting a remedy, Mr. Howard travelled into fome of the neighbouring counties in fearch of a precedent. In this fearch, fcenes of calamity and injuftice ftill opening upon him, he went on, and paid vifits to moft of the county gaols in England. Some peculiarly deplorable objects coming in his view, who had been brought from the Bridewells, he was induced to enter upon an examination of thefe places of confinement ; for which purpofe he travelled again into the counties he had before feen, and into all the reft, vifiting Houfes of Correction, City and Town Gaols.

He had carried on thefe inquiries with fo much affiduity, that fo early as March 1774, he was defired to communicate his information to the Houfe of Commons, and received their thanks. As he was then little known, I cannot much wonder that fo extraordinary an inftance of pure and active benevolence was not univerfally comprehended even by that patriotic body; for a member thought fit to afk him " at whofe expence he travelled ?" a queftion which Mr. Howard could fcarcely anfwer without fome indignant emotions. Soon after this public teftimony given to the exiftence of great abufes and defects in our prifons, a very worthy member, Mr. Popham, brought into the Houfe two bills, one " for the relief of acquitted prifoners in matter of fees"—the other " for preferving the health of prifoners."— Thefe falutary acts paffed during the fame feffion, and made a commencement of thofe reforms which have fince been fo much extended. Mr. Howard, aware of the great deficiency of the mode of promulgating laws among us, had thefe acts printed in a different character, and fent to every keeper of a county-gaol in England!

In this year he was induced, by the urgent perfuafions of his neighbours and friends of the town of Bedford, to ftand candidate, in conjunction with Mr. Whitbread, to reprefent that borough in parliament. No two perfons could be better entitled to the efteem of a town; and they were very warmly fupported in a conteft, which however terminated in the return of two other gentlemen. Mr. Whitbread and Mr. Howard petitioned the Houfe againft the return; and the event was, that the former, and one of the fitting members, were declared duly elected. To thofe who are acquainted with the conftitution of that borough, it will not appear extraordinary, that a perfon poffeffing the attachment of a majority of the inhabitant voters fhould lofe his election. This, however, was a moft fortunate circumftance for the public; fince, if Mr. Howard had obtained a feat in the Houfe of Commons, his plans for the reformation of prifons, muft have been brought within a narrow compafs; and the collateral inquiries, which, fo greatly to the advantage of humanity, he afterwards adopted, could never have exifted.

It was Mr. Howard's intention to have publifhed his account of Englifh Prifons in fpring 1775; but as he was fenfible, that to point out defects, without at the fame time fuggefting remedies, would be of little advantage, he thought it beſt to examine with his own eyes, what had been actually put in practice with reſpect to this part of police, in ſome of the moſt enlightened countries on the continent. Accordingly, in that year he viſited France, Flanders, Holland, and Germany ; and in 1776 repeated his viſit to thoſe countries, and alſo went to Switzerland. In the intervals he made a journey to Scotland and Ireland, and reviſited the county-gaols and many others in England.

Thus furniſhed with a ſtock of information greater than had ever before been collected on this ſubject ; and, indeed, probably greater than any man had, in the ſame ſpace of time, ever collected on any ſubject that required ſimilar pains ; he offered it to the public in 1777 in a quarto volume of near 500 pages, dedicated to the Houſe of Commons, by way of grateful acknowledgment for the honor conferred on him by their thanks, and for the attention they had beſtowed on the buſineſs. Before I proceed to give an account of this work, I ſhall juſt obſerve, that ſo zealous was Mr. Howard to diffuſe information, and ſo determined to obviate any idea that he meant to repay his expences by the profitable trade of Book-making, that, befides a profufe munificence in prefenting copies to all the principal perfons in the kingdom, and all his particular friends, he infifted on fixing the price of the volume fo low, that, had every copy been fold, he would ftill have prefented the public with all the plates, and great part of the printing. And this practice he followed in all his fubfequent publications ; fo that, with literal propriety, he may be faid to have GIVEN them, to the world. By the large expences of his journey, charities and publications, he has made himfelf even a greater pecuniary benefactor to mankind than can readily be paralleled in any age or country, his proportioned circumftances confidered. Yet how fmall a part was this of the facrifices he made !

He chofe the prefs of Mr. Eyres at Warrington, induced by various elegant fpecimens which had iffued from it, and by the opportunity a country prefs afforded, of having the work done under his own infpection, at his own time, and with all the minute accuracy of correction he determined to beftow on it. I may alfo fay, that an opinion of the advantage he might there enjoy of fome literary affiftance in the revifion and improvement of his papers, was a farther motive. To this choice I was indebted for that intimate perfonal acquaintance with him, which I shall ever esteem one of the most honourable circumstances of my life, and the lively recollection of which will, I trust, never quit me while memory remains. He refided in Warrington during the whole time of printing, and bis attention to bufinefs was moft indefatigable. During a very fevere winter he made it his practice to rife at three or four in the morning, for the purpofe of collating every word and figure of his daily proof sheet with the original.

As I thought it right to mention Mr. Howards literary deficiencies, it is become neceffary to inform the public of the manner in which his works were compofed. On his return from his tours he took all his memorandum-books to an old retired friend of his, who affifted him in methodizing them, and copied out the whole matter in correct language. They were then put into the hands of Dr. Price, from whom they underwent a revifion, and received occafionally confiderable alterations. What Mr. Howard himfelf thought of the advantages they derived from his affiftance, will appear from the following paffages in letters to Dr. Price. " I am " afhamed to think how much I have accumu- " lated your labors, yet I glory in that affift- " ance to which I owe fo much credit in the " world, and, under Providence, fuccefs in " my endeavours." ———" It is from your " kind aid and affiftance, my dear friend, " that I derive fo much of my character and " influence. I exult in declaring it, and " fhall carry a grateful fenfe of it to the laft " hour of my exiftence."—With his papers thus corrected, Mr. Howard came to the prefs at Warrington; and firft he read them all over carefully with me, which perufal was repeated, fheet by fheet, as they were printed. As new facts and obfervations were continually fuggeft- ing themfelves to his mind, he put the matter of them upon paper as they occurred, and then requefted me to clothe them in fuch expreffi- ons as I thought proper. On thefe occafions, fuch was his diffidence, that I found it diffi- cult to make him acquiefce in his own lan- guage when, as frequently happened, it was unexceptionable. Of this additional matter, fome was interwoven with the text, but the greater part was neceffarily, thrown into notes, which in fome of his volumes, are nume- rous.

The title of this first work is, *The State of the Prisons in England and Wales ; with preliminary Observations, and an Account of some Foreign Prisons.* It begins with a general View of Distress in Prisons, shewing in what respects those of England are deficient in the articles of food, water, bedding, and fresh air ; and that the morals of the prisoners are totally neglected, the most criminal and abandoned being suffered to corrupt the younger and less practiced. Notice is also taken of the gaol-fever, a disease which has in a peculiar manner infested the prisons of this country, and has at various times spread its ravages from them among our courts of judicature, our fleets, and armies. The author's next section is on Bad Customs in Prisons, under which he takes notice of the demand of garnish, the permission of gaming, the use of irons, the practice of varying the towns where the assizes are held, the local unfrequency of gaol-delivery, the fees still demanded by clerks of assize and of the peace, the non-residency of gaolers, the crowding of gaols with the wives and children of prisoners, and the circumstance of some gaols being private property. From this, and the foregoing section, every one must be convinced of the dreadful ſtate of our police in this important matter, and the abſolute neceſſity for a reformation. For proof that the complaints here made in general terms are not unfounded or exaggerated, he properly refers to the ſubſequent account of particular gaols, where they are too abundantly verified. He concludes the ſecond ſection with an enumeration of all the priſoners in England and Wales, under their ſeveral claſſes, who, in 1776, amounted to 4084, a number much leſs than ſome vague conjectures had ſtated, yet ſufficiently great to demand the ſerious attention of the legiſlature, eſpecially when it is conſidered that every man in priſon may be reckoned to have two dependents on him for ſupport.

Mr. Howard's third ſection offers propoſed Improvements in the Structure and Management of Priſons. He begins with obſervations on the priſon itſelf, with reſpect to its ſituation and plan, the latter of which is illuſtrated by an engraving. He then proceeds to that moſt eſſential topic, the regulations. Theſe he conſiders under the ſeveral heads of gaoler, chaplain, ſurgeon, fees, cleanlineſs, food, bedding, rules and orders, and inſpector. He much inſiſts upon the neceffity of abfolutely taking away the tap from the keepers of prifons, the poffeffion of which was obvioufly the caufe of promoting intemperance and riot, from the intereft it gave the keeper in fuch irregularities. In lieu of this fource of profit, he propofes a liberal addition to the falaries of this officer, the importance and refpectability of whofe employ he every where inculcates. He makes a feparate article of Bridewells, the original penitentiary-houfes of the country, and planned with much wifdom, but which, by long neglect and abufe, were become rather a nuifance than an advantage to the police. In many of them, though the perfons confined were fentenced to hard labour, no work of any kind was done; and this ftate of idlenefs, with the company of hardened criminals, proved to be a moft effectual method of completing the corruption of young and petty offenders. Various excellent remarks and fuggeftions are given in the whole of this fection, which contains the ground-work of all improvement in the economy of prifons and houfes of correction.

In fect. IV. Mr. Howard gives an account of Foreign Prifons; not of all he had feen, but of fuch only as afforded matter of inftruction; nor in thefe does he notice the frauds and defects he obferved, for he fays, "the redrefs and inveftigation of foreign abufes was not my object." The countries of which the prifons are defcribed are France, Switzerland, Germany, Holland, and Flanders. In the firft, the fufpicious policy which then prevailed would have rendered it very difficult for him to have obtained accefs to the interior part of the prifons, had he not availed himfelf of a benevolent rule, which permits any perfon to diftribute alms to the prifoners with his own hands. A fpirit of order and precifion, tempered with humanity, was obfervable in the conduct of this department, the regulations of which were fixed by a very comprehenfive and judicious code contained in an arret of 1717. In Switzerland, the feparation of male and female prifoners, the folitary confinement of felons, and the employment of thofe called galley-flaves, are circumftances deferving notice. The German prifons are regulated in a fimilar manner; and the houfes of correction at Manheim, Hamburgh, and Bremen, afford ufeful examples of order and induftry. But it is in Holland that the purpofe of reforming crimi-

nals by a courfe of difcipline is carried into execution with moft care and effect. Few debtors and
few atrocious offenders are to be found there ;
and the rafp and fpin-houfes contain the great body of prifoners. The regulations of thefe are given in detail, and the different employments of
the prifoners in different towns are particularly noted. Holland appears to be Mr. Howard's great fchool, to which we fhall fee that
he was never wearied in returning. The
Auftrian Netherlands offer fome of the largeft
eftablifhments of the penitentiary kind, and
prove the poffibility of managing a great number of criminals fo as to make them ufeful to
the ftate, and decent in their behaviour, by
the aid of fteady difcipline and feparate confinement at night. Mr. Howard faw, what
I fuppofe was then deemed an impoffibility in
England, in the houfe of correction at Ghent,
near 190 ftout criminals governed with as
much apparent eafe as the moft fober and
well-difpofed affembly in civil fociety. The
regulations of this prifon are defervedly given
at fome length. Mr. Howard concludes this
fection with a forcible and manly appeal to
his countrymen with refpect to the comparifon
he was obliged to exhibit between foreign and
Englifh police in this point, fo unfavourable to

E

the latter; calling upon his reader to judge, from the facts laid before him, " whether a defign of reforming our prifons be merely vifionary; and whether idlenefs, debauchery, difeafe, and famine, be the neceffary attendants of a prifon, or only connected with it in our ideas, for want of a more perfect knowledge and more enlarged views."

Section V. takes up the greateft part of the book. It contains a particular account of Englifh prifons, arranged according to the circuits, and comprifing every county in England and Wales. The mode adopted is very well contrived for the eafy confultation of magiftrates and other perfons concerned. Every principal prifon in London, and every county and city gaol, has the leading facts refpecting it difpofed in a fhort table under the four heads of gaoler, prifoners, chaplain, and furgeon. A brief defcription follows of fituation, plan, meafurements, &c. with fuch remarks, either of approbation or cenfure, as the circumftances fuggefted. Lifts are given of legacies and benefactions; and all tables of fees, and rules and orders, are copied *verbatim.* Next to thefe, are concife accounts of all the county Bridewells, and the town gaols and

Bridewells, with occasional remarks. The work is closed by some tables relative to fees and numbers, crimes and punishments of criminals. A short conclusion terminates the whole, in which the author apologizes for the language of censure he has so often been compelled to use, enumerates the leading objects requiring reform, and promises. that if such a thorough parliamentary enquiry into this great object, as alone can prove effectual to put it upon a proper footing, should be undertaken, he would devote his time to a more extensive foreign journey, for the sake of obtaining new information to lay before the public.

I cannot dismiss the account of Mr. Howard's first and great work, without a few reflections, to which the contemplation of it gives rise. And first, we may derive from it a clear idea of the capital objects which the author had at heart respecting prisoners These were, to alleviate their miseries, and correct their vices. As to the former purpose, he considered that men, partaking a common nature, have certain claims upon their fellow-creatures which nothing can entirely abrogate :—that even the highest degree of criminality does not abfolutely exclude compaffion towards the perpetrators of crimes, efpecially when fuffering under their effects;—that as no man paffes through life without fome deviation from ftrict rectitude, fo none has lived without the performance of fome good actions —and that, although human laws muft draw a line between fuch circumftances of conduct as do, or do not, come within their cognizance, yet there is a tribunal before which all mankind muft appear as culprits, only diftinguifhed by the degree of delinquency. He further confidered, that among the inmates of a prifon there is every poffible degree of moral demerit, from the mere inconfiderate violation of fome hard, ill-underftood, local law, to the deliberate breach of the moft facred and univerfal rule of action; and that a great number are, in the eye of the law, innocent perfons, only under a temporary ftate of confinement, till their conduct is properly inveftigated. From thefe different views of the fubject, he convinced himfelf, that it was the duty of every fociety to pay due attention to the health, and, in fome degree, even to the comforts, of all who are held in a ftate of confinement;—that wanton and unneceffary rigour fhould be practifed upon none;—and that fome were entitled to all the indulgencies compatible with their condition. It was, however, by no means his wifh (as fome chofe to reprefent it) to render a prifon fo comfortable an abode, that the l■■■rder of fociety might find their conditio■■■■ bettered by admiffion into it. On the contrary, the fyftem of difcipline which he defired to eftablifh, was fuch as would appear extremely grievous to thofe of an idle and licentious difpofition. For, whenever imprifonment was made the punifhment of a crime, his idea of reformation became a leading principle in the regulation of prifons; and it was that which coft him the chief labour in collecting and applying facts. To accomplifh this end, he fhewed that thefe things were effential ;—ftrict and conftant fuperintendence—clofe and regular employment —religious inftruction—rewards for induftry and good behaviour, and penalties for floth and audacioufnefs—diftribution into claffes and divifions according to age, fex, delinquency, &c.—and occafional and nocturnal folitude. In laying down thefe regulations, he might be thought to have given way to a certain aufterity, were it not fo tempered by attention to : the real demands of human nature, and fanc- · tified by a regard to the beft interefts of ef. ·

fenders themselves, that the friend of mankind was ever apparent, even in the strict disciplinarian. He extremely lamented that the plan of reformation seemed, of all parts of his system of improvement, least entered into or understood in this country : The vulgar idea that our criminals are hardened and abandoned beyond all possibility of amendment, appeared to him equally irrational and pernicious. He scorned, through negligence or dispair, to give up the worst cases of mental corruption ; he fully believed that proper remedies, duly administered, would recover a large share of them ; and he thought it the greatest of cruelties to consign a soul to perdition, without having made every effort for retrieving it. Merely to get rid of convicts by execution or perpetual banishment, he regarded as a piece of barbarous policy, equally denoting want of feeling, and deficiency of resource ; and he had not so much English prejudice about him, as to suppose, that a system not adopted in this country was therefore absurd or impracticable.

My second to of reflection is the striking proof this work affords of the extensive benefit arising from a free press. By its means we see an individual, enjoying neither royal nor ministerial patronage, but solely borne up by ardent zeal for the public good, and the resources of his own mind and fortune, enabled not only to lay before the world complete information concerning a most important and little known subject, but, in some measure, also to enforce the correction of abuses, by bringing before the bar of the public those by whose negligence or criminality they had been fostered. For as the history of mankind has shewn on the one hand, that palpable injustice and mismanagement, even in an absolute government, cannot long stand their ground against the odium of an enlightened public ; so, on the other, it has proved, that even in free constitutions, notwithstanding all their boasted checks and balances, very gross abuses may long prevail, unless they are placed in open day, and submitted to the censure of the nation at large. It is scarcely, I think, to be doubted, that the freedom we enjoy in this country, and the ultimate defeat of every pernicious project, are less owing to the mechanism of our constitution, than to the habitual practice (rather assumed by the spirit of the people than granted by the laws) of subjecting every public measure to popular discussion by means of the press.

From this ready communication of facts and opinions, it has happened, that many useful designs and improvements have among us originated from persons who had neither power nor interest of their own, but whose plans were adopted in consequence of the public conviction. The respect paid to Mr. Howard's virtues, abilities, and industry, placed him in a manner at the head of the department in which he had engaged as a volunteer; and this, not only in his own country, but afterwards, in some measure, throughout Europe. Though in exercising the office of a censor he was superior to the fear of giving offence, yet he ever observed the utmost delicacy in marking out individuals as objects of blame. He boldly and forcibly displayed the abuse, but left it to those more immediately concerned, to take notice of the delinquent. It cannot be questioned, that numbers looked with an evil eye upon his keen researches and free detections; but how could they venture, before the public, to confront a man whose assertions were correct, whose intentions were above all suspicion, and whose life would stand the severest test? May this example animate all future friends of mankind with a noble confidence becoming their cause?

The House of Commons now took up, with, laudable zeal, the important business of regulating the prisons; and in the draught of a bill "to punish by imprisonment and hard labour certain offenders, and to establish proper places for their reception," the plan was formed upon the Rasp and Spin Houses in Holland. Mr. Howard was now called upon by his promise, as well as his inclination, to make a new tour for the purpose of acquiring fresh and more exact information. He, accordingly, in April 1778, went over to Holland, and revisited with the greatest attention the well-conducted establishments of the penitentiary kind in the United Provinces. Thence he travelled into Germany, taking his course through Hanover and Berlin, to Vienna. From this capital he proceeded to Italy by Venice; and, having gone as far south as Naples, returned by the western side of that country to Switzerland. Thence he pursued the course of the Rhine through Germany; and, crossing the Low Countries to France, returned to England in January 1779. During the spring and summer of this year he made another complete tour of England and Wales, and likewise took a journey through Scotland and Ireland.

The labours of thefe two years were certainly not lefs productive of ufeful information
than his former journeys. In fome refpects
they were more valuable, fince, being now
fully matter of his fubject, and acquainted with
the means of procuring the beft intelligence,
he purfued his inquiries with greater eafe and
effect. He was now, too, a diftinguifhed character in Europe, and might venture to affume
that kind of authority, to which the collection
of facts, interefting to all civilized nations,
feemed to entitle him. It is here proper to
mention, that although he often found it neceffary, efpecially when treading new ground,
to avail himfelf of recommendations to perfons
high in rank and office ; yet that he much preferred, when he could practife it, carrying on
his refearches as an unknown individual, whofe
bufinefs was not fufpected, and who took fuch
times and opportunities of making his vifits, as
fecured him againft any thing like difguife or
preparation. And it was his general cuftom,
after he had once obtained accefs to a prifon
by the prefence and interpofition of authority,
to ftay fome time in the place, or revifit it, for
the purpofe of renewing his enquiries fingle
and unexpected. Thus careful was he to guard
againft deception ; and with fuch coolnefs of

investigation did he execute a design which it required so much ardour of mind to conceive.

I shall not, however, conceal, that some, sensible and not uncandid observers of his conduct have thought him too apt to be prejudiced by first impressions, the effects of which it appeared extremely difficult to remove; and they have also charged him with sometimes giving undue credit to persons of inferior condition, at the places where he was making his inquiries; and likewise with being apparently better pleased with finding occasion to censure than to commend. If, in a few instances, there may have been grounds for these imputations (as nothing human is without its defects), yet I think his works may, on the whole, be confidently referred to, as proving, by an immense mass of allowed and uncontradicted facts, the accuracy of his representations. It is likewise to be considered, that, as abuses in general proceed from superiors, it was not likely that a fair account of them should be obtained from that quarter: and, as his great purpose was to correct, it is natural that his attention should have been more drawn to what was wrong than what was right. A Hercules who went about in order to contend with monfters, had little to do with the fair forms of civil life. Yet numerous inftances of liberal praife may be found in his works, ef-pecially where he could propofe the object of it as an example proper for imitation.

The tours now before us were likewife ren-dered richer in utility by the comprehenfion of another great object, that of hofpitals. To thefe inftitutions of humanity Mr. Howard had long been attached; he had been a pro-moter of them, and attentive to their improve-ment; and in his journies through this king-dom, he had feldom failed to vifit the hofpi-tals and infirmaries fituated in our principal towns. He had alfo, in his firft publication, taken curfory notice of a few which he faw abroad. But he now made them an avowed object of his examination; a circumftance, it may be fuppofed, not a little pleafing to his medical friends. For, although the knowledge collected by a profeffional man with fimilar opportunities would, doubtlefs, have been more applicable to the purpofe of fcience, yet matter of fact, accurately ftated by a fenfible obferver, muft ever have its value. Befides, when can we expect to fee the fpirit and qualities of a Howard, united, in one of our profeffion, with his fortune and leifure?

The fruit of all this refearch appeared in the year 1780, in an Appendix to the State of the Prifons in England and Wales ; containing a further account of foreign Prifons and Hofpitals, with additional remarks on the Prifons of this country. It is a quarto volume of about two hundred pages, with feveral plates. The work begins with the foreign prifons and hofpitals, and Holland takes the lead, fince a main object of the journey was a minute account of the excellent regulations of the houfes of correction in that country. Many of the rules, dietaries, &c. are copied ; and on quitting the country, Mr. Howard gives his teftimony to the large field of information on this fubject that it affords, and fays, that he knows not which moft to admire, " the neatnefs and cleanlinefs appearing in the prifons, the induftry and regular conduct of the prifoners, or the humanity and attention of the magiftrates and governors." He takes little notice of the hofpitals for the fick in Holland, not approving their mode of keeping patients fo warm, and excluding the frefh air. At Berlin the re-

gularity and strictness of the police shews the ruling spirit of the great Frederic. A workhouse here is conducted in the best Dutch mode. Vienna affords little to commend in its prisons; on the contrary, its horrid dungeons seem the abode of the extremest human misery. Scarcely any thing in Mr. Howards descriptions is more touching than the following picture :—
" In one of the dark dungeons, down twenty-four steps, I thought I had found a person with the gaol-fever. He was loaded with heavy irons, and chained to the wall: anguish and misery appeared with tears clotted on his face. He was not capable of speaking to me; but, on examining his breast and feet for Petechiæ, or spots, and finding a strong intermitting pulse, I was convinced that he was not ill of that disorder. A prisoner in an opposite cell told me, that the poor creature had desired him to call for assistance, and he had done it, but was not heard*." The charities of this

* This scene is the subject of the frontispiece to Mr. Haley's Ode to Mr. Howard; and it is better drawn in the following stanza of that performance.

Where in the dungeon's loathsome shade
The speechless captive clanks his chain,
With heartless hope to raise that aid
His feeble cries have call'd in vain:

city, chiefly founded by' the late Emprefs Queen, are much more pleafing fubjects of defcription.

Mr. Howard entered Italy with high expectations of improvement from its numerous charitable inftitutions and public edifices; nor does it appear that he was altogether difappointed, as this country affords him a pretty long and interefting article. The governments in which a fpirit of improvement and attention to public objects, feem moft to prevail, are thofe of Milan and Tufcany. The hofpitals in Italy afford fome novelties and ufeful hints; but there appears to be a great difference among them as to cleanlinefs and good management. Rome and Milan have well conducted houfes of correction, of which plans and defcriptions are given. In a room of the former is infcribed a fentence, which fo admirably expreffed Mr. Howard's idea concerning the purpofe of civil policy relative to criminals, that he would, I believe, almoft have thought

Thine eye his dumb complaint explores;
Thy voice his parting breath reftores;
Thy cares his ghaftly vifage clear
From death's chill dew, with many a clotted tear,
And to his thankful foul returning life endear.

it worth while to have travelled thither for that alone. PARUM EST COERCERE IMPROBOS POENA, NISI PROBOS EFFICIAS DISCIPLINA. *It is doing little to restrain the bad by punishment, unless you render them good by discipline.* The galleys belonging to various states in Italy, and used for punishment, may be usefully compared with our HULKS.

The western side of Germany offers some good regulations in its houses of correction; but in general, the police of this country is no object of imitation. The dungeons of Liege present pictures to the imagination, more dreadful, if possible, than those of Vienna. "In descending deep below ground," says Mr. Howard, "I heard the moans of the miserable wretches in the dark dungeons. The sides and roof were all stone. In wet seasons, water from the fosses gets into them, and has greatly damaged the floors."——"The dungeons in the new prison are abodes of misery still more shocking; and confinement in them so overpowers human nature, as sometimes irrecoverably to take away the senses. I heard the cries of the distracted as I went down to them." Surely the Liegois cannot be blamed for endeavouring to place civil authority in different hands from thofe who thus outraged the feelings of human nature!

The additional notices of France are diftinguifhed by an account of the Baftille, extracted from a fcarce pamphlet, which Mr. Howard procured, not without hazard, and a tranflation of the whole of which he likewife printed. He had reafon to believe, that this expofure to all Europe of the horrid fecrets of this "prifon-houfe," was a caufe that his after vifits to that country were attended with no fmall danger to his liberty; and it was once not improbable that Mr. Howard fhould have been in the number of thofe victims whom the demolition of that fortrefs of defpotifm reftored to light and freedom. What a triumph muft it have been to him, to have learned, that the frowning towers, which could not be approached or even gazed at, without offence, were levelled to the ground, as the firft facrifice to the recovered rights of a generous nation! It is remarkable, that France was of all countries that in which he found intelligence concerning the prifons and other government eftablifhments, moft difficult to be obtained; and this union of the fufpicious rigour of the police with the exterior gaiety and frivolity of the national character,

gave him no fmall difguft. It is to be prefumed, that the change in their conftitution will
foften this contraft into a defirable harmony between the principles of the adminiftration and
the manners of the people.

Great Britain being then at war with
France, Spain, and America, Mr. Howard
could not be unmindful of that clafs of honourable prifoners to which he himfelt had once be-
longed. He very attentively vifited the Englifh prifoners of war confined in Calais and
French Flanders, noting down their complaints
and all the particulars of their treatment. He
alfo, as I have been well informed, clothed at
his own expence, feveral who had been fhip-
wrecked on the French coaft in the dreadful
ftorm of December 31, 1778, and were left
almoft naked. He likewife exerted himfelf in
diffuading the men from enlifting with the
French, who were endeavouring to feduce
them ; by which he greatly offended the perfons in office there, who could not imagine
that he acted in all this as a private man, but
were ftrongly perfuaded that he was a fecret
agent or fpy of the Englifh government. This
natural fuppofition may ferve as fome apology

for the fufpicion and illiberality with which he was conftantly treated in that country.

On his return to England, with the true fpirit of a citizen of the world, he paid immediate vifits to the French, Spanifh, and American prifoners of war in this country; nor did he forget thole in Scotland and Ireland. The refults of his obfervations, given with the moft perfect impartiality, fucceed the account of foreign prifons and hofpitals; and it cannot be doubted that they had confiderable effect in alleviating the unavoidable hardſhips of war.

Mr. Howard next gives a brief account of what he obferved worthy of notice in his tours through Scotland and Ireland. The former country being governed by a different fyftem of municipal law from that of England, afford fome ufeful remarks concerning imprifonment for debt, the form of adminiftering an oath, and the mode of conducting executions. Ireland has not been at all behind-hand with the fiſter kingdom in paffing acts for the liberal improvement of its prifons; but there did not, at that time, appear an equal attention in magiftrates to put them in execution. Some remarks here introduced, concerning the practice of recruiting the army out of the gaols, will be thought important by thofe, who wifh that the clafs of armed citizens fhould be re-fpectable, in proportion to its confequence.

The next article relates to the Hulks on the Thames. Thefe, at their firft inftitution, had been extremely unhealthy, in confequence of faults which Mr. Howard pointed out in his former work. Their ftate was now much mended by means of parliamentary interfe-rence; yet, on the whole, it was not a mode of imprifonment and employment which met with his approbation. Some further remarks on the Gaol-fever fucceed; which, in addition to the general caufes of want of frefh air and cleanlinefs, he attributes to fuch a fudden change of diet and lodging as breaks the fpi-rits of convicts. This correfponds with the medical doctrine of the effect of debilitating caufes, in producing fevers of the typhus kind; yet it feems fuch a caufe as cannot well be avoided.

The remainder of the book is occupied by a frefh furvey of the prifons in England and Wales, in which fuch changes as had taken place fince his former publication are noted, with occasional observations. The reader will remark with pleasure, that in most parts of the kingdom, various useful alterations had been made since the period in which Mr. Howard began his enquiries; and the great share he had in occasioning them will be universally admitted.

His conclusion expresses satisfaction with the result of his labours; and mentions, that it had been his intention now to retire to the tranquil enjoyment of that competence Providence had bestowed on him, but that the earnest persuasions of those who thought him a proper person to superintend one of the great plans he had so much recommended, had induced him still to devote his time to the public. Concerning this matter, it is proper to enter into an explanation. I shall only first mention, that, together with this Apendix, there was printed a new edition, in octavo, of the State of the Prisons, with which all this additional matter was interwoven.

An act for establishing Penitentiary Houses, on which much labour and thought had been bestowed by men of great ability, passed in

1779. By this act, three supervisors were appointed for the purpose of superintending the execution of the buildings. The whole kingdom would naturally turn its eyes on Mr. Howard, as the first person whose services should be engaged on this occasion; but it was not an easy task to obtain his acquiescence. Among other objections, his extreme delicacy, with respect to pecuniary emolument, stood in his way; and even the moderate salary annexed to this office, seemed to him scarcely compatible with the absolute disinterestedness of conduct he had maintained, and was determined to preserve, during the whole of his labours. At length, however, the solicitations of his friends, particularly of the late Sir W. Blackstone, the great promoter of the design, together with a consciousness of the service he might render the public in this station, overcame his reluctance. Having resolved to accept of no salary for himself, and having made the association of his highly-respected friend, Dr. Fothergill, a condition of his compliance, he, with the Doctor, and Mr. Whately, treasurer of the Foundling-hospital, were nominated by his Majesty as the three supervisors. The first matter for their determination was, fixing on the ſpot where the two penitentiary houſes for the metropolis ſhould be erected. Various ſituations were propoſed, and Mr. Howard paid due attention to all the plans, by viſiting the ſpots, and maturely conſidering all circumſtances favourable and objectionable. The reſult was, that his opinion and that of Dr. Fothergill coincided in giving a preference to Iſlington, for reaſons which he has ſtated in his laſt publication. Mr. Whately preferred the ſituation of limehouſe. By the death-bed advice of Sir W. Blackſtone, the two friends adhered to their opinion; but the matter was made an affair of obſtinate contention, and remained undecided during the year 1780. At the end of it Dr. Fothergill died; upon which event, Mr. Howard, foreſeeing that the want of the ſupport of ſuch a colleague would render his future interference uſeleſs, ſent his reſignation of the office of ſuperviſor in January 1781, in a letter to Earl Bathurſt, which he has printed.

Now that Mr. Howard had freed himſelf from the engagement, which ſeemed to be the only obſtacle between him and that elegant retreat which for ſo many years he had inhabited, it might naturally be imagined that he would

fit down in repofe, for the remainder of his
life, fatisfied with the unparalleled and fuccefsful exertions he had made for the relief of the
moft diftreffed portion of mankind ; and thenceforth employ himfelf only in thofe more confined deeds of beneficence which he had ever
practifed. But it was a leading feature in his
character, not to be content with any thing
fhort of the greateft perfection, which every
object of his purfuit was capable of attaining—
and this principle could fcarcely fail of applying
itfelf to a fubject fo important as that which
had for fome years occupied his attention.—
Though his refearches in thofe foreign countries which promifed moft information, might
have been fuppofed to have exhaufted that
fource of improvement, yet, on furveying fo
large a tract of Europe as yet unvifited, he
could not be fatisfied to remain unacquainted
with the ufeful facts relative to his purpofe,
which might poffibly lie there concealed. And
he was convinced, that every new vifit, even
to places already examined, would afford new
inftruction..

. It was therefore no furprife to thofe who
intimately knew him, to learn, that in the
fummer of 1781 he was fet out on a tour to

the capitals of Denmark, Sweden, Ruffia, and Poland, with the further intention of revifiting Holland and part of Germany. From this tour he returned towards the clofe of the year. I have before me a letter of his to a friend (the Rev. Mr. Smith, of Bedford, dated Mofcow, September 7, 1781, whence it appears, that thefe parts of the world were lefs fuitable to his mode of living than the countries through which his former travels lay. " I thought (fays he) I could live where any man did live ; but this northern journey, efpecially in Sweden, has pinched me : no fruit, no garden-ftuff, four bread, four milk :—but in this city I find every luxury, even pine-apples and potatoes." He mentions having declined every honour that was offered him at Peterfburgh, even that of a foldier to attend him on his journey ; and fays, that he will not leave Mofcow, till he has made repeated vifits to the prifons and hofpitals, fince the firft man in the kingdom had affured him, that his publication would be tranflated into Ruffian.

The year 1782 he was employed in another complete furvey of the prifons in England, and another journey into Scotland and Ireland.— The Irifh Houfe of Commons having appointed a gaol-committee, he reported to it the ftate of feveral of the prifons in Dublin. Other objects in that Ifland alfo engaged his attention, of which an account will be given hereafter.

Spain and Portugal yet remained untouched ground. Confidering how much the fpirit of religious bigotry and civil defpotifm has thrown thefe countries back in the progrefs of modern improvement, much inftruction was not to be expected from them ; yet the very circumftance of their difference from the reft of Europe made their fyftems of police an object of curiofity. He failed to Lifbon in February 1783, and proceeded thence by land into Spain, paffing from Badajos to Madrid, and through Valladolid, Burgos, and Pamplona, to France. From this laft country he returned through Flanders and Holland to England. Travelling in Spain is a fevere trial of patience to thofe who have been accuftomed to eafy conveyance and luxurious indulgencies ; but Mr. Howard's wants were eafily fatisfied. " The Spaniards, (fays he, in a letter to the fame friend) are very fober, and very honeft ; and if a traveller can live fparingly, and lie on the floor, he may pafs tolerably well through their country." From Lifbon to Madrid he could feldom get

the luxury of milk with his tea ; but one morning (he tells his friend) he robbed a kid of two
cups of its mother's milk. He remained, however, in perfect health and spirits ; and received that mark of attention which he moſt of all
valued, a free acceſs to the priſons of all the
cities he viſited, by means of letters to the ma-
giſtrates from Count Campomanes.

After a ſhort repoſe on his return from this
tour, he made another journey in the ſummer
of the ſame year into Scotland and Ireland,
and again viſited ſeveral of the Engliſh priſons.

His materials had now once more accumulat-
ed to ſuch a maſs, as to demand communicati.
on to the public. During the laſt three years
his labours had been even greater than in any
former equal period ; yet it could not be expected, that the matter abſolutely new which
he had collected ſhould be proportionally great.
It was however, enough, to employ him very
cloſely during ſeveral months of the year 1784,
in printing an Appendix, and a new edition of
the main work, in which all the editions were
compriſed. The Appendix contains all the
matter of that of 1780, together with what

had fince accrued. Of the latter I now proceed to give fome account.

Several new houfes of correction are defcribed under the head of Holland, the country which Mr. Howard ever found the moft
fertile fource of inftruction in this branch of
police. The plan of the large new work-
houfe of Amfterdam muft be well worth ftu-
dying, as affording hints for the conftruction
of penitentiary houfes. Germany has the addition of the prifons of Hanover and Bremen,
a minute account of the great and well regulated work-houfe at Hamburg, and fhort notices concerning Silefia. Of the northern
kingdoms which he now firft vifited, it may in
general be obferved, that their models, as well
with refpect to police, as to mode of living,
have been Holland and Germany; but their
poverty, and the rigour of their climate, have
made them degenerate in their imitations. In
particular, they are extremely deficient in
cleanlinefs and induftry. The new articles,
therefore, of Denmark and Sweden, though
valuable for the information they contain, yet
afford little or nothing of inftruction. The
vaft empire of Ruffia, lately emerged from ob-
fcurity to take a commanding ftation in the

fyftem of Europe, and governed by uncontroled power, at prefent directed by a fpirit of
magnificent improvement, could not but offer
in its inftitutions various things worthy of notice. Its police refpecting criminals, its prifons, hofpitals, and places of public education,
are briefly mentioned by Mr. Howard; but he
has found little to propofe as an example for o-
ther countries. The regulations of the great
convent at Peterfburgh, for the education of
female children of the nobility and common-
ers, are given in detail, and afford fome falutary rules for the prefervation of the health of
young perfons, and for promoting habits of
cleanlinefs and temperance. The plan and
defcription of a magazine for medicinal herbs
at Mofcow, will be a pleafing novelty to moft
readers. Mr. Howard had been anticipated
in his furvey of the prifons and hofpitals of the
northern kingdoms, by that well-informed
traveller, Mr. Coxe, who publifhed a pamphlet
on the fubject in 1781, here referred to with
commendation. The fhort head of Poland contains little but a teftimony to the neglected
and wretched ftate of public inftitutions in that
ill-governed country. All travellers have
concurred in fimilar reprefentations of the
whole fyftem of affairs, internal and external,

in that unhappy feat of ariftocratical tyranny ;
fo that it may be prefumed, their does not exift fo determined an enemy of innovation as not
to rejoice in the change of conftitution which
has lately been effected there, by means of the
filent and peaceable progrefs of light and reafon.

There are various additional articles under
Flanders, one of which relates to a great alteration for the worfe in the houfe of correction at Ghent. A once flourifhing manufactory carried on in the prifon was at an end ; and
the allowance of victuals to the prifoners was
reduced in quantity and quality. In the account of a very offenfive prifon at Lille, Mr.
Howard expreffes his grateful acknowledgments to Providence for his recovery from a
fever caught there of the fick.

The account of Portugal is almoft confined
to the prifons and hofpitals of Lifbon ; the ftate
of which, upon the whole does credit to the
government. The employment of about a
a thoufand vagrant and deferted children in
a manufactory, is one of the moft obfervable
circumftances.

SPAIN, which has been long diſtinguiſhed for its charitable eſtabliſhments, affords like-wiſe in its criminal police, many things deſerv-ing of attention; though the ſpirit of rigour and ſeverity is perhaps too apparent, amidſt much laudable order and exactneſs. The houſe of correction at Madrid, called San Fernando, may vie with ſome of the beſt regulated inſti-tutions of this nature; and the Hoſpicio, a kind of work-houſe, in which extenſive manu-factories are carried on, is a good example of the union of employment with confinement.— The account of the charitable ſociety of the Hermandad del Refugio, who patrole the ſtreets in the evening, for the purpoſe of invit-ing deſtitute wanderers to a comfortable ſup-per and night's lodging, will excite pleaſing ſenſations in the breaſt of every lover, of hu-manity. The priſons of the inquiſition, thoſe objects of horror and deteſtation to every Pro-teſtant, and now, probably, to moſt Catholics, excited great curioſity in Mr. Howard, of which however, all his efforts could only pro-cure a partial gratification. Yet he has been able to communicate enough concerning thoſe of Valladolid to form a ſtriking picture of ter-ror. On the whole, the predilection he had long entertained for the Spaniſh character, was not diminifhed by his vifit to the country ; nor does he feem to have thought his pains in extending his inquiries to it, ill beftowed. The additional notices in France, chiefly relate to the Paris hofpitals. It is needlefs to dwell on thefe, fince a very accurate defcription of them has fince been given in a capital work by M. Tenon.

To the account of foreign prifons and hofpitals, fucceeds a frelh furvey of the prifoners of war.

The new journies to Scotland, now extended as far as Invernefs, afford little but cenfure for the neglect of the prifons in that country. Under Ireland are introduced additional remarks on the faults and abufes ftill obfervable in the prifons there. Notwithftanding a very fpirited exertion of the legiflature to amend their ftate, by framing good acts for their regulation. But, " quid leges fine moribus, &c." The horrid effects of that cheap poifon, whifky, upon the health and morals of the lower claffes in that country, are noticed by Mr. Howard with much indignant difguft. A new object of attention occurred to him in the two laft vifits to Ireland,—the Proteftant Charter

Schools, a noble foundation, but which he found funk into wretched abufe, notwith-standing the patronage and fuperintendance of the firft perfons in that kingdom. Erroneous accounts of them, publifhed by a committee, and authorized by being annexed to a printed fer-mon of a prelate in their favour, were detected by Mr. Howard on his vifits to fome of them, and are expofed with his ufual freedom.

⌐ Further accounts of the Hulks follow. To the remarks on the gaol-fever, Mr. Howard adds the information, that in 1782 he did not find one perfon in this kingdom affected with that difeafe ; but that in 1783 he had the mortification to obferve feveral prifons, thro' original bad conftruction and neglect, relapfing to their former ftate. So effential is a plan of conftant vigilance and infpection, to counteract the lamentable tendency to abufe in all public inftitutions ! This principle of corruption and decay in every thing human is fo inceffantly ac-tive, that, if not refifted by the timely efforts of reformation, all the contrivances of wifdom againft natural and moral evils, would, like the dykes of Holland, perpetually fapped and worn by the force of the elements, fall into irremedi-able ruin.

The remainder of this volume is taken up with a review of all the Englifh prifons, together with particulars of all the alterations which they had undergone fince the laft publication. The reader will be gratified in finding, from the number of new prifons, and new buildings and conveniencies added to the cld, that the counties in general had by no means been deficient in liberal attention to this great objeft, fince it had been brought forward and aided by Mr. Howard's indefatigable exertions. At the conclufion, among the tables, is a fketch of general heads of regulations for penitentiary-houfes, which will be highly ufeful in fuggeft-ing a complete body of rules and orders for fuch eftablifhments, if ever they fhould again be thought of in this country.

The printing of this copious Appendix, together with a complete edition of his State of the Prifons, into which all the additions were incorporated, making a large and clofely print-ed quarto volume, occupied much of Mr. Howard's time in the year 1784. The re-mainder of that, and the greater part of the next year, do not appear marked with his public fervices. They were, I believe, chief-ly employed in domeftic concerns, of which the choice of a proper place of education for his fon, now rifing towards manhood, was one that moft interefted him. But the habitude of carrying on refearches into an object, which by long poffeffion had acquired deep root in his mind, together with a new idea, collaterally allied to it, which had ftruck him, at length impelled him once more to engage in the toils and perils of a foreign journey.

He had obferved that, notwithftanding the regulations for preferving health in prifons and hofpitals, infectious difeafes continued occafionally to arife and fpread in them : he had alfo in his travels remarked the great folicitude of feveral trading nations to preferve themfelves from that moft deftructive of all contagious diftempers, *the Plague;* and, at the fame time, he was well apprized of the rude and neglected ftate in which the police of our own country is left refpecting that object. Combining thefe ideas, he thought that a vifit to all the principal Lazarettos, and to countries frequently attacked by the plague, might afford much information as to the means of preventing contagion in general, as well as particular inftruction concerning eftablifhments for the purpofe of guarding againft peftilential infection. His intent, therefore, was nothing lefs, than to plunge into the midft of thofe dangers which by other men are fo anxioufly avoided ; to fearch out and confront the great foe of human life, for the fake of recognizing his features, and difcovering the moft efficacious barriers againft his affaults. Who but muft be ftruck with admiration of the firmnefs of courage, and the ardour of benevolence, which could prompt fuch a defign! As a proof of his own idea of the hazards he was to encounter, it may be mentioned, that he refolved to travel fingle and unattended ; not thinking it juftifiable to permit any of his fervants to partake of a danger to which they were not called by motives fimilar to his own.

It was towards the end of 1785 that Mr. Howard fet out upon this tour, taking his way through Holland and Flanders, to the fouth of France. As, from the jealoufy and difpleafure of the French government, he was not able to obtain permiffion to vifit the eftablifhments there, or even to gain affurance of perfonal fafety, he travelled through the country as an Englifh phyfician, never took his meals in public, and entrufted his fecret only to the proteftant minifters. In a letter from Nice to the friend above-mentioned, dated January 30, 1786, he acquaints him with thefe circumftances, and fays, that he was five days at Marfeilles and four at Toulon; and, as it was thought that he could not get out of France by land, he embarked in a Genoefe veffel, and was feveral days ftriving againft wind and tide. They who at prefent conduct the government of France, I am perfuaded, will blufh at the idea, that a Howard was obliged to conceal his name and purpofe while carrying on in their country inquiries which had no other aim than the good of mankind!

From Nice, Mr. Howard went to Genoa, Leghorn, and Naples, and to the iflands of Malta and Zante. He then failed to Smyrna, and thence to Conftantinople. I have been favored with a letter of his to Dr. Price from this metropolis, dated June 22, 1786, fome extracts from which I fhall prefent to the reader.

" After viewing the effects of the earthquake in Sicily, I arrived at Malta, where I repeatedly vifited the prifons, hofpitals, poorhoufes, and lazarettos, as I ftaid three weeks.

H

From thence I went to Zante : as they are all Greeks, I wifhed to have fome general idea of their hofpitals and prifons, before I went into Turkey. From thence, in a foreign fhip, I got a paffage to Smyrna. Here I boldly vifited the hofpitals and prifons ; but as fome accidents happened, a few dying of the plague, feveral fhrunk at me. I came thence about a fort-night ago. As I was in a miferable Turk's boat, I was lucky in a paffage of fix days and a half. A family arrived juft before me, had been between two and three months.

" I am forry to fay fome die of the plague about us ; one is juft carried before my win-dow ; yet I vifit where none of my conductors will accompany me. In fome hofpitals, as in the lazarettos, and yefterday among the fick flaves, I have a conftant headach, but in about an hour after it always leaves me. Sir Ro-bert Ainflie is very kind ; but for the above and other reafons, I could not lodge in his houfe. I am at a phyfician's, and I keep fome of my vifits a fecret."

He defigned to proceed from Conftantinople over land to Vienna ; but, having determined, upon reflection, to obtain by perfonal experi-

ence the fulleft information of the mode of performing quarantine, he returned to Smyrna,
where the plague then was, for the purpofe of
going to Venice with a foul bill, that would
neceffarily fubject him to the utmoft rigor of
the procefs. His voyage was tedious, and
rendered hazardous by equinoctial ftorms; and
in the courfe of it he incurred a danger of
another kind, the fhip in which he was a paf-
fenger being attacked by a Tunifian corfair,
which, after a fmart fkirmifh, was beaten off
by the execution done by a cannon loaded with
fpike nails and bits of iron, and pointed by Mr.
Howard himfelf. It afterwards appeared to
have been the intention of the captain to blow
up his veffel, rather than fubmit to be taken into perpetual flavery. • It was not till the clofe
of 1786 that Mr. Howard left his difagreeable
quarters in the lazaretto of Venice, in which
his health and fpirits fuffered confiderably.
Thence he went by Triefte to Vienna. In
this capital he had the honor of a private con--
ference with the Emperor, which was conducted with the utmoft eafe and condefcenfion on
the part of Jofeph II. and equal freedom on
the part of the Englifhman. A relation of
this inftructive fcene in his own words, will, I
doubt not, be agreeable to the reader : " The

Emperor defired to fee me, and I had the honor of a private audience with him of above an
hour and an half. He took me by the hand
three times in converfation, and thanked me
for the vifit. He afterwards told our Ambaffa-
dor, ' That his countryman fpoke well for prifoners; that he ufed no flowers, which others
ever do, and mean nothing.' But his greateft
favor to me was his immediate alterations for
the relief of the prifoners*." That the late
Emperor had an ardent zeal for improvement
of every kind, and a ftrong defire of promoting the profperity of his fubjects, will fcarcely
be denied, even by thofe who are the fevereft
cenfurers of the mode in which he conducted
his plans, and his extreme mutability refpecting them. He will alfo be honored, for the
readinefs with which he laid afide the etiquette
of his rank, on every occafion where it ob-
ftructed him in the acquifition of knowledge, or
the activity of exertion. Mr. Howard returned through Germany and Holland, and arrived fafe in England early in 1787.

It was during this tour, and while he was in
folitude occupying a cell of the Venice lazaret-

* Letter to Mr. Smith.

to, that he received from England two pieces
of intelligence, both of which diftreffed and
harraffed his mind, though the emotion they
excited muft apparently have been very different. One of thefe related to the melancholy
derangement of mind into which his fon had
fallen, and which, after various inftances of
ftrange and unaccountable behaviour, terminated at length in decided infanity. They who
cannot believe that the moft benevolent of
mankind could be a ftern and unnatural parent,
will fympathize in the anguifh he muft have felt
on hearing (and in fuch a fituation too) of an
event which blafted the deareft hopes of comfort and folace in his declining years. I, who
have frequently heard him fpeak of this fon,
with all the pride and affection of the kind father of an only child, cannot read without
ftrong emotions, the expreffions he ufes in writing to his friend ralative to this bitter calamity. When he concludes a long letter upon various topics, with the exclamation, " But, O !
my fon, my fon!" I feem to perceive the efforts of a manly mind, ftriving by the aid of
its internal refources to difpel a gloomy phan-
tom, which was yet ever recurring to his imagination. But in this emergency, as in all

others, the confolations of religion were his chief refuge*.

The other caufe of uneafinefs by which his mind was agitated, will, to many, appear a very extraordinary one ; fince it arofe from a teftimony of efteem and veneration in his countrymen, which might be imagined to afford balm for his wounded fpirit. During his abfence, a fcheme had been fet on foot to honor him in a manner almoft unprecedented in this age and country. Without attempting to trace it to its origin, it may fuffice to fay, that, in a periodical work of extenfive circulation, the public were called upon to teftify their refpect for Mr. Howard by a fubfcription, for the pur-

---

* To prove that Mr. Howard had kind and tender feelings for domeftic as well as for public occafions, will I hope, by moft perfons be deemed a fuperfluous tafk. For thofe who require fuch proof, I copy the following paffage from one of his letters to Mr. Smith. "My old fervants, John Prole, Thomas Thomafon, and Jofeph Crockford, have had a fad time. I hear they have been faithful, wife, and prudent. Pleafe to thank them particularly in my name for their conduct. Two of them, I am perfuaded, have acted out of regard to his excellent mother,—who, I rejoice, is dead." —

pofe of erecting a ftatue, or fome other monument, to his honor. The authors of this
fcheme, though, doubtlefs, actuated by a pure
and laudable admiration of illuftrious virtue,
yet muft have been totally unacquainted with
Mr. Howard's difpofition ; otherwife they
would never have thought of decorating a
man, whofe characteriftic feature had always
been a folicitude to fhun all notice and diftinction, with one of the moft glaring and promi-
nent marks of public applaufe, which might
put to the blufh modefty of a much lefs delicate texture than his. The Englifh national
character (if national character can be faid to
belong to fo heterogeneous a people) is by nothing fo ftrongly marked, as by a coynefs and
referve which fhrink from obfervation, and
even to thofe who are acting for the public,
render the gaze of the public eye painful. The
love of glory, which is fo active a fentiment
to fome of our neighbours, operates feebly
upon us : many do not rife to it, and fome go
beyond it. That " humble Allen," whofe
difpofition it was to " do good by ftealth and
blufh to find it fame," was a genuine Englifh
philanthropift ; and fuch was Mr. Howard,
rendered, perhaps, ftill more averfe to public

praise, by a deep fenfe of religious humility.

A fimilar want of acquaintance with Mr.
Howard's defigns, caufed the propofers of this
plan to attribute to him an extravagance of
philanthropy, which could not but appear ri-
diculous to thofe whofe judgment was not daz-
zled by the ardor of admiration. It was afferted, among real topics of applaufe, that he
was now gone abroad with the view of extir-
rating the plague from Turkey; an idea fcarcely fo rational, the character of that nation confidered, as would be that of a miffion to con-
vert the Grand Seignior to Chriftianity. Mr.
Howard meant, undoubtedly, to do all the
good which fhould lie within his compafs in
that, as in all other countries which he vifited;
but he never was fo romantic as to fuppofe that
he could effect that, which would manifeftly
require a total change in the religious and political fyftem of a great empire, of all the leaft
difpofed to change.

The project of a ftatue, however, was eager-
ly adopted; the fubfcription filled, and was
adorned with the names of minifters, nobles,
and perfons of diftinction : and a committee

was appointed to determine upon the beſt mode
of fulfilling its purpoſe. The confidential
friends of Mr. Howard were in a diſagreeable
dilemma ; for as, on the one hand, they could
not but rejoice in the warmth of admiration
which his country teſtified for his character ;
ſo, on the other, they well knew that its manner of diſplay could not fail to give him extreme pain, and if effected, probably baniſh
him forever. On this account, they did not
concur in the ſcheme, and ſome of them ven-
tured publicly to throw out objections to it.
Some of its warm promoters, in reply, talked
of *forcing his modeſty,* and ſeemed determined
at all events to put in execution their favorite
deſign. In the mean while, Mr. Howard was
informed of this honorable perſecution that
was preparing againſt him at home ; and the
ſenſations this intelligence occaſioned in his
breaſt are ſhewn in the following expreſſions
contained in a letter to the intimate friend who
has already furniſhed me with various extracts.
" To haſten to the other very diſtreſſing affair : oh, why could not my friends, who know
how much I deteſt ſuch parade, have ſtopped
ſuch a haſty meaſure !—As a private man, with
ſome peculiarities, I wiſhed to retire into ob-
ſcurity and ſilence.—Indeed, my friend, I can-

not bear the thought of being thus dragged
out. I immediately wrote, and hope fomething may be done to ſtop it. My beſt friends
muſt diſapprove it. It deranges and confounds
all my ſchemes—my exaltation is my fall, my
misfortune*." The ſame ſentiments on this
buſineſs are expreſſed with equal ſtrength in
his letters to Dr. Price. Among other things
he ſays, "My trueſt, intimate, and beſt friends,
have, I ſee by the papers, been ſo kind as not
to ſubſcribe to what you ſo juſtly term a haſty
meaſure. Indeed, indeed, if nothing now can
be done, I ſpeak from my heart, never poor
creature was more dragged out in public."

That in all this there was no affectation,
clearly appeared from the letter he ſent to the
ſubſcribers; in which, after expreſſing his gratitude, he diſplayed ſo determined a repug-
nance againſt admitting of the propoſed honor,
deprecating it as the ſevereſt of puniſhments,

* He mentions in the ſame letter, as a proof how
oppoſite his wiſhes were to monumental honors, that
before he ſet out on this journey, he had given directions, that in caſe of his death, his funeral expences
ſhould not exceed ten pounds—that his tomb ſhould be a
plain ſlip of marble placed under that of his dear Henrietta in Cardington church, with this inſcription:
John Howard, died—aged—My hope is in Chriſt.

that nothing could be urged in reply, and the bufinefs was dropped. Of the fum fubfcribed, amounting to upwards of 1500*l.* Mr. Howard refufed to direct the difpofal in any manner, and begged it might no longer be termed the *Howardian fund.* A part of it was reclaimed by the fubfcribers, but a confiderable fhare remained in a ftock ; and, fince Mr. Howard's death, it has been refolved to employ it in conferring thofe honors on his memory which he would not accept while living. This intention is in every refpect ftrictly proper ; and, as the noble edifice of St. Paul's is at length deftined to receive national monuments, no commencement can be more aufpicious, than with a name which will ever ftand fo diftinguifhed among thofe,

Qui fui memores alios fecere merendo.

To refume the narrative of Mr. Howard's publiq life :—After his return in 1787, he took a fhort repofe, and then went over to Ireland, and vifited moft of the county gaols and charter fchools, and came back by Scotland. In 1788 he renewed his vifit to Ireland, and completed his furvey of its gaols, hofpitals, and fchools. I fhall lay before the reader part of a letter to Dr. Price, dated from Dublin, March

23, of this year. " My journey into this country was to make a report of the ſtate of the charter ſchools, which charity has been long neglected and abuſed; as indeed moſt public inſtitutions are made private emoluments, one ſheltering himſelf under the name of a biſhop, another under that of a lord ; and for electioneering intereſt breaking down all barriers of honor and honeſty. However, Parliament now ſeems determined to know how its grants have been employed. I have, ſince my viſits to theſe ſchools in 1782, been endeavouring to excite the attention of Parliament; and ſome circumſtances being in my favor, a good Lord Lieutenant, a worthy Secretary (an old acquaintance,) and the firſt Secretary of State, the Provoſt, a ſteady friend, I muſt ſtill purſue ; ſo I next week ſet out for Connaught and other remote parts of this kingdom, which indeed are more barbarous than Ruſſia. By my frequent journies my ſtrength is ſomewhat abated, but not my courage or zeal in the cauſe I am engaged in." During theſe two years, he likewiſe repeated his examination of all the county gaols, moſt of the Bridewells, and the infirmaries and hoſpitals of England, and of the hulks on the Thames, at Portfmouth and Plymouth*.

The great variety of matter collected in thefe journies was methodized and put to the

---

*It was, I believe, during his abfence in fome of the tours of this period, that an incident happened which the reader, I hope, will think well worth relating. A very refpectable-looking elderly gentleman on horfe-back, with a fervant, ftopt at the inn nearest Mr. Howard's houfe at Cardington, and entered into converfation with the landlord concerning him. He obferved, that characters often appeared very well at a diftance, which could not bear clofe infpection; he had therefore come to Mr. Howard's refidence in order to fatisfy himfelf concerning him. The gentleman then, accompanied by the innkeeper, went to the houfe, and looked through it, with the offices and gardens, which he found in perfect order. He next enquired into Mr. Howard's character as a landlord, which was juftly reprefented; and feveral neat houfes which he had built for his tenants were fhewn him. The gentleman returned to his inn, declaring himfelf now fatisfied with the truth of all he had heard about Howard. This refpectable ftranger was no other than Lord Monboddo; and Mr. Howard was much flattered with the vifit, and praifed his Lordfhip's good fenfe in taking fuch a method of coming at the truth, fince he thought it worth his trouble.

I

prefs in 1789. It compofes a quarto volume,
beautifully printed, and decorated with a number of fine plates, which, as ufual, are prefented to the public; and fo eager were the pur-
chafers of books to partake of the donation,
that all the copies were almoft immediately
bought up. The title is, *An account of the
principal Lazarettos in Europe, with various papers relative to the Plague ; together with further obfervations on fome foreign Prifons and
Hofpitals ; with additional remarks on the prefent ftate of thofe in Great Britain and Ireland.*
Of this work I fhall proceed to give a brief
analyfis.

The firft fection relates to Lazarettos, beginning with that of Marfeilles, in which city
the horrid ravages of the plague, within the
prefent century, have left ftrong impreffions
of dread of that deftroyer of mankind. Thofe
of Genoa, Leghorn, Malta, Zante, Venice,
and Triefte follow ; the defcriptions of which
are illuftrated by excellent views and plans*.

* *In one of his letters, Mr. Howard mentions having met with a young Frenchman going to the academy
at Rome, who for a few fequins thankfully worked under his eye, fo that he can atteft the accuracy of his
draughts. Several of the plates were engraved in Holland.*

Of the lazarettos of Venice a very particular account is given, comprifing the mode of reception which he himfelf experienced, the regulations of every kind, refpecting officers and their duty, vifitation of fhips, manner of performing quarantine, and the expurgation of goods of all claffes, &c. All thefe appear to have been devifed with much judgment and prudence; but Mr. Howard is obliged to give teftimony to various inftances of abufe and neglect, which greatly impair the utility of this inftitution, as well as of many others in that once celebrated and potent republic.

Sect. II. contains propofed regulations, and a new plan for a lazaretto; followed by obfervations on the importance of fuch an eftablifhment in England. In thefe are introduced two letters on the fubject to Mr. Howard; one, a long and argumentative one from the Englifh merchants refiding at Smyrna; the other, confirming their opinion, from thofe of Salonica. Thefe commercial papers appear worthy of the moft ferious attention; and indeed it is wonderful that a nation which boafts of good fenfe and knowledge, fhould fo long have remained patient under a police refpecting this matter, which anfwers no effectual pur-

pofe of fecurity, but feems only calculated to
difcourage commerce, and produce fees to perfons in office, by the moft barefaced impofi-
tions*.

Sect. III. confifts of papers relative to the
plague. They commence with a fet of anfwers, by different medical practitioners, to
queries with which Mr. Howard was furnifhed
by the late Dr. Jebb and myfelf. I muft obferve, however, that all the queries do not appear, fome of them having been mifapprehend-
ed, or imperfectly anfwered, particularly fuch
as related to the difcrimination of other fevers
of the typhus genus from the plague. Thefe
replies will probably be thought to add little
to the ftock of knowledge we poffeffed refpecting this difeafe ; yet it is of fome importance,
that the leading facts on which all modes of
prefervation muft be founded, viz. that the
plague is not known to arife fpontaneoufly any
where, but is always to be traced to contagi-

---

* Such is the negligence and abfurdity refpecting the
regulations of the quarantine of perfons, that I have
been affured, a naval officer has been called out of the
Opera houfe, to go on board his fhip and perform his
quarantine.

on; and that the diſtance to which its infection extends through the atmoſphere is very ſmall, are eſtabliſhed in them by general agreement. The " Abſtract of a curative and preſervative method to be obſerved in Peſtilential Contagions," communicated from the Office of Health in Venice to the court of Ruſſia; and the " Abridged Relation of the Plague of Spalato in Dalmatia, in 1784." both extracted from the Italian originals by myſelf, are the other papers in this ſection. In the latter, the medical reader will be ſtruck with the equivocal nature of the ſymptoms ſuppoſed to diſcriminate this diſeaſe, and the very gradual progreſs from ſuſpicion to certainty as to its preſence.

Sect. IV. relates to foreign Priſons and Hoſpitals. The employment of the gally-ſlaves in the arſenal of Toulon, is the moſt obſervable circumſtance relative to the ſouth of France. Under Italy there is a pleaſing account of the improvements at Florence, in conſequence of the humane attention of the Grand Duke Leopold, the preſent Emperor. This prince, beſides other inſtances of liberal favor to Mr. Howard's inquiries, cauſed a copy of his new code of laws to be preſented to him, of which, on his return, Mr. Howard had a tranſlation

I 2

printed, and diftributed among the heads of the law and other perfons, in and out of Parliament. Of the Grand Duke Mr. Howard never fpoke without the warmeft expreffions of gratitude and refpect, calling him a glorious prince, and declaring that nothing could exceed his attention to whatever might promote the happinefs and profperity of his people. It is earneftly to be wifhed, that the fame regard to the principles of juftice and humanity may accompany him in the very elevated ftation which is now affigned him by Providence.

Malta, that celebrated feat of piracy, dignified by the fpirit of chivalry and devotion, affords a new and curious article. Its great hofpital, which boafts of lodging the fick in a palace, and ferving them in plate, is here defcribed by one whofe penetrating eye could diftinguifh between parade and comfort; and it undergoes fome fevere cenfure. Mr. Howard vifited it before he delivered his letter of recommendation from Sir W. Hamilton to the Grand Mafter, as well as frequently afterwards.

The Turkifh dominions, whence all light, liberty, and public fpirit, are moft effectually

excluded, could not be expected to yield inftruction in police to Europe. Yet debtors
and felons are there confined in feparate prifons, a refinement to which this country is not
yet entirely arrived. The hofpitals in the great
commercial city of Smyrna feem all to belong to
the Franks, Greeks, and Jews. Even at Conftantinople the Turks have few hofpitals, and
thofe in a wretched ftate. The hofpitals for
lunatics there, are, indeed, examples of ad-
mirable conftruction, but neglected in their
management. Yet, amidft this difregard of
the human fpecies, Mr. Howard found an
afylum for cats. Such are the contradictions
of man !

The inftitutions of Vienna fhew that fingular mixture of clemency and rigour, of care and
neglect, that might be expected from the inde-
cifive character of the fovereign. The perpetual confinement of criminals in dark, damp
dungeons, as a fubftitute for capital punifhment, manifeftly appears to be as little an advantage on the fide of lenity, as it is on that of
public utility. The much beaten ground of
Holland ftill affords new obfervations, particularly refpecting the legal procefs for debt, in
ufe there.

Sect. V. relates to Scotland; and what is new chiefly regards the charitable inftitutions of Edinburgh. As to the prifons there, Mr. Howard was obliged to remark to the Lord Provoft, "that the fplendid improvements carrying on in their places of entertainment, ftreets, fquares, bridges, &c. feemed to occupy all the attention of the gentlemen in office, to the total neglect of this effential branch of the police." This weighty animadverfion deferves ferious notice, as a ftrong confirmation of thofe charges againft the fpirit of luxury, which various modern philofophers have been fond of turning into ridicule. In fact, a fpirit which increafes perfonal wants and indulgencies, and augments the diftance between the higher and lower orders of fociety, cannot but interfere with the duties, as well of charity, as of juftice, which are owing to our fellow-creatures of every condition. The arts of luxury may promote knowledge, and this may fecondarily be employed with advantage on objects of general utility; but it is not likely that the fame perfons whofe minds are occupied with fchemes of fplendor and elegant amufement, fhould beftow attention on the coarfe and difgufting offices annexed to the care of the poor and miferable.

The subject of Sect. VI. is the Irish Prisons and Hospitals. Mr. Howard observed a very liberal and humane spirit with respect to prisons, prevailing among the gentlemen of that country, displayed in the erection of many new gaols, the plans of which, however, he could not approve. The evils occasioned by the use of spiritous liquors, particularly apparent in Ireland, draw from him much complaint and censure. It is a shocking consideration that the interest of the revenue should, in this matter, be suffered to prevail over the good of the nation; and nothing can deserve severer animadversion, than the conduct of those servants of the public, the commissioners of excise, who presume to grant licences to tippling houses in villages, contrary to the declared wish and opinion of gentlemen who reside on the spot, and are witnesses of their fatal consequences to the health and morals of the neighbourhood. This is indeed, reversing the order of civil government, and elevating subaltern interests to ruling principles. All the hospitals in Dublin are noticed by Mr. Howard, with remarks. He then proceeds to a survey of all the county gaols and hospitals in the kingdom. The-county hospitals are in fact national institutions, maintained in great part by the county rates and king's letter, and therefore are not fo exactly fuperintended as thofe in England, which depend upon private fubfcription for their fupport. The confequence of this is fhewn in the wretched ftate in which the greater part of them were found; the abodes of filth, hunger, neglect, and every fpecies of abufe. Yet a fpirit of improvement was beginning to operate among them, to which this free ftatement of their defects would, doubtlefs, mueh contribute.

Sect. VII. is devoted to an account of the Charter-fchools in Ireland. The public detection of mifreprefentations and abufes in this great national object had excited the attention of feveral of the leading men ; and Mr. Howard had been defired to lay his obervations before the committee of fifteen in Dublin, who have the fuperintendance of them. He alfo made a report of their ftate before the Irifh Houfe of Commons ; and, having entered heartily into the fubject, he refolved to give it a thorough invefligation. He therefore extended his vifits to the whole of them, in number thirty-eight, and to the four provincial nurferies from which they are fupplied. The refult of his obfervations is here given, with free

cenfures of defects, and candid acknowledgments of improvement. He concludes the account with fome general remarks on the inftitution, and fome hints for rendering it more
ufeful ; and, after expreffing a wifh, that the
benefits of education were more generally extended over Ireland than they can be by thofe
fchools, he difplays the enlarged liberality of his
mind in the following fentence, which contains
a maxim worthy of being written in letters of
gold. " I hope I fhall not be thought, as a Proteftant diffenter, indifferent to the Proteftant
caufe, when I exprefs my wifh, that thefe diftinc-
tions(between Catholic and Proteftant)were lefs
regarded in beftowing the advantages of education ; and that the increafe of Proteftantifm
were chiefly trufted to the diffemination of
knowledge and found morals."

This fection is concluded, with an example
ftrikingly illuftrative of the eafe with which
education may be extended to the whole body
of poor, afforded by the truftees of the blue-
coat-hofpital in Chefter, whofe report of their
plan and its fuccefs is here copied: and alfo,
with the rules of the Quaker's-fchool at Ack-
worth, excellently adapted to promote that
decent and regular deportment in youth which

Mr. Howard fo much admired. Ireland has reafon to think herfelf peculiarly indebted to him for his laborious inveftigations and free remarks on her public inftitutions. No country certainly wanted them more; and none, I believe, is better difpofed to profit by them. She has not been ungrateful to her benefactor (that was never her character) for in no country is the memory of Mr. Howard more revered. During his journies there, feveral of the principal towns prefented him with their freedom; and the Univerfity of Dublin, with great liberality, conferred on him the honorary degree of Doctor of Laws. Mr. Howard's averfion to all kinds of diftinction, and the natural diflike of changing his ufual defignation at an advanced age, prevented him from publicly affuming this refpectable title.

Sect. VIII. relates to Englifh Prifons and Hofpitals. The prifons are all fpecified in the order of the former works, with fuch remarks as the alterations made in them, and other circumftances, fuggefted. Many of the defcriptions of hofpitals are new, particularly an account of all the hofpitals for the fick in the metropolis. It is probable that few inftitutions of the kind in Europe are better conducted than thefe ; yet there are defects, both general and particular, which Mr. Howard has briefly pointed out, and which claim the attention of thofe who are really interefted in the utility of thefe noble charities, and do not confider them merely as fubfervient to private emolument. In a note under the county gaol in Southwark, he mentions in ftrong terms of pity and indignation the ftate of fifty felons, fentenced for tranfportation in the courfe of the preceding five years, and kept in the moft wretched condition till an opportunity fhould offer of putting their fentence in execution. This neceffary delay of punifhment muft ever be a ftrong objection to the fcheme of diftant banifhment, and gives a decided preference, both in juftice and policy, to the plan of penitentiary houfes, fo thoughtlefsly abandoned for the Botany-bay fettlement. The injuftice, indeed, of the intermediate confinement, is leffened by an act of 24th Geo. III. which directs, that all the time during which a convict fhall have continued in gaol under fentence of tranfportation, fhall be deducted out of the term of his tranfportation. Still, however, fuch confinement is a different, and, in thefe circumftances, a much worfe, punifhment, than that to which they are fentenced.

K

The county Bridewell at Reading occasions a note which deserves particular attention. Mr. Hôward has been suppofed the peculiar patron of folitary confinement, and his recommendation has caufed it to be adopted in various places, but to a degree beyond his intentions. He well knew, from manifold obfervation, that human nature could not endure, for a long time, confinement in perfect folitude, without finking under the burden. He had feen the moft defperate and refractory in foreign countries tamed by it; he therefore propofed in our own prifons a temporary treatment of this kind, as the moft effectual, yet lenient, mode of fubduing the ferocity of our criminals : but he never thought of its being made the fentence of offenders during the whole term of their imprifonment ; fuch being not only extreme and fcarcely juftifiable feverity, but inconfiftent with the defign of reclaiming them to habits of induftry by hard labour. He, indeed, univerfally approved of nocturnal folitude, as affording an opportunity for ferious reflection, and preventing thofe plans of mifchief, and mutual encouragements to villainy, which are certain to take place among criminals, when left to herd together without infpection.

The employment of convicts in building a new county gaol at Oxford, with their general good behaviour in it, affords an example of the poſſibility and probable good effect of occupying them in uſeful labour at home.

The fever wards of the Cheſter infirmary are very properly noticed, as a ſpirited inſtance of extending relief to perſons fuffering under a dangerous and infectious difeafe, and, by proper regulations, rendering the contagion harmleſs to others. I am perfuaded, that the plague itſelf, thus managed, might be prevented from communicating itſelf even to thoſe under the fame roof with it. Mr. Howard was happy to find in this city a character congenial with his own in the ardour of active benevolence, and diſtinguiſhed by various fuccefsful plans for the public good. To the medical reader, as well as to many others, it will be unneceſſary to mention the name of Dr. Haygarth.

A particular account of all the hulks is given at the end of the Engliſh gaols. The condition of theſe floating Bridewells was improved in ſeveral reſpects ſince Mr. Howard's former viſits; but, if conſidered in any other light than as temporary places of confinement till some better plan is adopted, they are liable to many objections, which are here stated.

Remarks on Penitentiary Houses follow. In these the writer states his ideas concerning their nature and object, gives the reasons which induced Dr. Fothergill and himself to fix on the situation of Islington, and relates his resignation of the office of Supervisor, as formerly mentioned. The general heads of regulations proposed for such houses in the last Appendix, are here reprinted ; and a plate is added explanatory of the plan of building he approves. It is on every account to be lamented, that Mr. Howard should not have had the satisfaction of seeing one of his favourite designs, the subject of his most laborious research and maturest reflection, carried into execution. The objection of expence was surely unworthy of a country like this, whose prosperity and resources are so magnificently displayed, when the provinces of Holland, petty states of Germany, and cantons of Switzerland, have not been afraid of incurring it. Whether the preferred scheme of colonizing with convicts at the Antipodes, has the advantage of it in this respect, the public are now pretty well able to determine.

In the remarks on the gaol fever, repeated with a little variation from the laft publication, we are informed, that fince 1782, when the prifons of this kingdom were entirely free from this difeafe, feveral fatal and alarming inftances of it had occurred. Its appearance and frequency will probably much depend upon the epidemic conftitution of the year, as long as its occafional caufes continue to fubfift; but that proper care and regulations in prifons might almoft entirely extirpate thefe caufes, there feems no reafon to doubt.

The conclufion expreffes the writer's fatisfaction in that humane and liberal fpirit which has fo much alleviated the diftrefs of prifoners; but laments, that here its exertions feem to ftop, and that little or nothing is done towards that moft important object, the reformation of offenders. From clofe obfervation he is convinced, that the vice of drunkennefs is the root of all the diforders of our prifons, and that fome effectual means to eradicate it are neceffary, if we mean to preferve the health and amend the morals of prifoners. Mr. Howard therefore fubjoins, as his final legacy towards the improvement of this branch of police, the draught of a bill for the better regulation of gaols, and the prevention of drunkennefs and rioting in them. Of this, the leading claufes are framed for the purpofe of abfolutely prohibiting the entrance of any liquor into a gaol except milk, whey, buttermilk, and water, unlefs in cafe of ficknefs and medical prefcription. He was fully fenfible that, in this free living country, the denial of even fmall beer would be deemed a fpecies of cruelty ; and he doubted not that it would go far to lofe him, in the popular eftimation, the title of the *Prifoner's Friend:* but as attaining a popularity of that kind was not his original objeft, fo he could bear to forfeit it, while confcious of ftill purfuing the real good of thofe unhappy people. Being convinced from experience, that there was no medium in this matter, and that if ftrong liquors were at all admitted into prifons, no bounds could be fet to their ufe, he thought it right to deny an indulgence to a few, for the fake of the effential advantage of the many. Debtors, then, while the fame place of confinement ferve for them and felons, muft be fubjected to the fame reftraints. And, to take off the objeftion of the hardfhip this would im-

pofe upon innocent debtors, it was greatly his
wifh, that fuch alterations fhould take place in
our law for debt, that none but fraudulent
debtors fhould be liable to imprifonment, who,
he juftly obferves, are really criminals. He
fuppofes that the gentlemen of the faculty will
condemn the total rejection of fermented liquors from the diet of prifoners, under the notion of their being ufeful as antifeptics; and I
confefs I was one who pleaded with him on
this fubject: but he anfwered me with argu-
ments which he has here ftated, and they are
worthy of confideration. After all, many will
fuppofe, that in his feelings, both with refpect
to thefe privations, and to his propofed indulgencies of tea, and other vegetable articles, he
was in fome meafure under the influence of his
own peculiar habits of life; fo natural is it for
our judgment of particulars to be warped, when
our general principles remain fixed and unal-
tered. The draught of a bill will, I prefume,
appear in moft refpects excellent; and the great
purpofe of preferving fobriety in gaols, cannot,
furely, be too much infifted on.

Mr. Howard's leading ideas on this fubject
were formed fome years before. In May
1787, the Lord Chancellor, in an excellent

speech on a propofed Infolvent Bill, after difcuffing the point of imprifonment for debt, and the nature of fuch bills, proceeded to fome confiderations refpecting the management and difcipline of our prifons. He faid, "he had lately had the honor of a converfation upon the fubject, with a gentleman who was, of all others, the beft qualified to treat of it—he meant, Mr. Howard, whofe humanity, great as it was, was at leaft equalled by his wifdom; for a more judicious, or a more fenfible reafoner upon the topic, he never had converfed with. His own ideas had been turned to folitary imprifonment and a ftrict regimen, as a punifhment for debt; and that notion had exactly correfponded with Mr. Howard's, who had agreed with him, that the great object ought to be, when it became neceffary to feclude a man from fociety, and imprifon him for debt, to take care that he came out of prifon no worfe a man in point of health and morals than he went in." His Lordfhip afterwards recited a ftory which Mr. Howard had told him, in proof of the corruption and licentioufnefs of our prifons. A Quaker, he faid, called upon him to go with him and witnefs a fcene which, if he were to go fingly, would, he feared, be too much for his feelings: it was, to vifit a friend in diftrefs—a perfon who had lately gone into the King's-bench prifon. When they arrived, they found the man half-drunk, playing at fives. Though greatly fhocked at the circumftance, they afked him to go with them to the coffee room, and take a glafs of wine. He refufed, faying he had drank fo much punch, that he could not drink wine—however, he would call upon them before they went away. Mr. Howard and his friend returned, with feelings very different from thofe with which they entered the place, but not lefs painful.

The volume concludes with feveral curious and valuable tables, which will probably be ufed for reference at future diftant periods. The enumeration of all the prifoners in England at his vifits in 1787 and 1788, fhews an alarming increafe, though in fome meafure to be accounted for, from a long fufpenfion of the ufual tranfportation. They amount to feven thoufand four hundred and eighty-two.

Mr. Howard remained but a fhort time at home after the printing of this work. In the conclufion of it he had declared his intention " again to quit his native country, for the pur-

pofe of revifiting Ruffia, Turkey, and fome
other countries, and extending his tour in the
eaft." The reafon he has affigned for this determination, is, "a ferious deliberate conviction that he was purfuing the path of his duty;"
and it cannot be doubted, that this confideration was now, as it ever had been, his leading
principle of action. But if it be afked, what
was his more peculiar object in this new journey, no decifive anfwer, I believe, can be given
by thofe who enjoyed the moft of his confidence. I had various converfations with him
on the fubject; and I found rather a wifh to
have objects of enquiry pointed out to him by
others, than any fpecific views prefent to his
own mind. As, indeed, his purpofe was to ex-
plore regions entirely new to him, and of which
the police refpecting his former objects was
very imperfectly known to Europe (for the
Turkifh dominions in Afia, Egypt, and the
Barbary coaft, were in his plan of travels), he
could not doubt that important fubjects for obfervation would offer themfelves unfought.
With refpect to that part of his tour in which
he was to go over ground he had already trod-
den, I conceive that he expected to do good in
that cenforial character, which his repeated
publications, known and attended to all over

Europe, gave him a right to affume ; and which
he had before exercifed to the great relief of
the miferable in various countries. If to thefe
motives be added the long formed habitude of
purfuing a certain track of enquiry, and an in-
quietude of mind proceeding from domeftic
misfortune, no caufe will be left to wonder
at fo fpeedy a renewal of his toils and dangers.

He had refolved to go this journey too,
without an attendant ; and it was not till after the moft urgent and affectionate entreaties,
that his fervant obtained permiffion to accompany him. Before he fet out, he and his very
intimate and highly refpected friend, Dr. Price,
took a moft affectionate and pathetic leave of
each other. From the age and infirmities of
the one, and the hazards the other was going
to encounter, it was the foreboding of each of
them that they fhould never meet again in this
world ; and their farewell correfponded with
the folemnity of fuch an occafion. The reader's mind will paufe upon the parting embrace
of two fuch men ; and revere the mixture of
cordial affection, tender regret, philofophic
firmnefs, and chriftian refignation, which their
minds muft have difplayed.

It was in the beginning of July 1789 that he arrived in Holland. Thence he proceeded through the north of Germany, Pruſſia, Courland, and Livonia, to St. Peterſburgh. From this capital he went to Moſcow. Some extracts of a letter to Dr. Price dated from this city, September 22, 1789, will, I doubt not, be acceptable, as one of the lateſt records of his career of benevolence.

" When I left England, I firſt ſtopped at Amſterdam, and proceeded to Oſnaburgh, Hanover, Brunſwick, and Berlin; then to Konigſberg, Riga, and Peterſburgh; at all which places I viſited the priſons and hoſpitals, which were all flung open to me, and in ſome, the burgomaſters accompanied me into the dungeons, as well as into the other rooms of confinement. I arrived a few days ago in this city, and have begun my rounds. The hoſpitals are in a ſad ſtate. Upwards of ſeventy thouſand ſailors and recruits died in them laſt year. I labour to convey the torch of philanthropy into theſe diſtant regions.——I am quite well— the weather clear—the mornings freſh—thermometer 48, but fires not yet begun. I wiſh for a mild winter, and then ſhall make ſome progreſs in my European expedition. My medical acquaintance give me but little hope of escaping the plague in Turkey. I do not look back, but would readily endure any hardships, and encounter any dangers, to be an honor to my Chriftian profeffion."

· From Mofcow he took his courfe to the very extremity of European Ruffia, extended as it now is to the fhores of the Black-fea, where long dreary tracts of defert are terminated by fome of thofe new eftablifhments, which have coft fuch immenfe profufion of blood and trea-fure to two vaft empires, now become neighbors and perpetual foes. Here, at the diftance of 1,500 miles from his native land, he fell a victim to difeafe, the ravages of which, among unpitied multitudes, he was exerting every effort to reftrain. *Finis vitæ nobis luctuofus, amicis triftis, extraneis etiam ignotifque non fine cura!*

From the faithful and intelligent fervant who accompanied him (Mr. Thomas Thomafon), I have been favored with an account of various particulars relative to his laft illnefs, which I fhall give to the reader in the form in which I received it.

L

"The winter being far advanced on the taking of Bender, the commander of the Ruffian army at that place gave permiffion to many of the officers to vifit their friends at Cherfon, as the feverity of the feafon would not admit of a continuance of hoftilities againft the Turks. Cherfon, in confequence, became much crowded; and the inhabitants teftified their joy for the fuccefs of the Ruffians by balls and mafquerades. Several of the officers, of the inhabitants of Cherfon, and of the gentry in the neighbourhood, who attended thefe balls, were almoft immediately afterwards attacked with fevers; and it was Mr. Howard's idea, that the infection had been brought by the officers from Bender. Amongft the number who caught this contagion was a young lady who refided about fixteen miles from Cherfon. When fhe had been ill fome little time, Mr. Howard was earneftly requefted to vifit her. He faw her firft on Sunday, December 27. He vifited her again in the middle of the week, and a third time on the Sunday following, January 3. On that day he found her fweating very profufely; and, being unwilling to check this by uncovering her arm, he paffed his under the bed-clothes to feel her pulfe. While he was doing this, the effluvia from her body were very offenfive to him, and it was always his own opinion that he then caught the fever. She died on the following day. Mr. Howard was much affected by her death, as he had flattered himfelf with hopes of her amendment. From January 3d to the 8th he fcarcely went out*; but on that day he went to dine with Admiral Montgwinoff, who lived about a mile and a half from his lodgings. He ftaid later than ufual; and when he returned, found himfelf unwell, and thought he had fomething of the gout flying about him. He immediately took fome Sal Volatile in a little tea, and thought himfelf better till three or four on Saturday morning, when feeling not fo well, he repeated the Sal Volatile. He got up in the morning and walked out ; but, finding himfelf worfe, foon returned and took an emetic. On the following night he had a violent attack of fever, when he had recourfe to his favorite remedy, James' powder, which he regularly took every two or four hours till Sunday the 17th. For though Prince Potemkin fent his own phyfician to him, immediately on being acquainted

---

* There feems fome miftake here, as there is a full report in his memorandums, of a vifit to the hofpitals in Cherfon, dated January 6.

with his illnefs, yet his own prefcriptions were
never interfered with during this time. On
the 12th he had a kind of fit, in which he fud-
denly fell down, his face became black, his
breathing difficult, and he remained infenfible
for half an hour. On the 17th he had another
fimilar fit. On the 18th he was feized with
hiccuping, which continued on the next day,
when he took fome mufk draughts by direction
of the phyfician. About feven o'clock on
Wednefday morning, the 20th of January, he
had another fit, and died in about an hour after. He was perfectly fenfible during his illnefs, except in the fits, till within a very few
hours of his death. This event he all along
expected to take place ; and he often faid, that
he had no other wifh for life than as it gave
him the means of relieving his fellow-creatures.

During his illnefs he received a letter from
a friend, who mentioned having lately feen his
fon at Leicefter, and expreffed his hopes that
Mr. Howard would find him better on his return to England. When this account was read
to him, it affected him much. His expreffions
of pleafure were particularly ftrong, and he
often defired his fervant, if ever by the bleffing

of God, his fon was reftored, to tell him how much he prayed for his happ.nefs. He made a will* on the Thurfday before he died; and was buried, at his own requeft, at the villa of M. Dauphine, about eight miles from Cherfon, where a monument is erected over his grave. He made the obfervation, that he fhould here be at the fame diftance from Heaven, as if brought back to England. While in Cherfon, he faw the accounts of the demolition of the Baftille, which feemed to afford him a very particular pleafure; and he thought it poffible, the account he had himfelf publifhed of it, might have contributed to this event."

On this relation, the general exactnefs of which may, I doubt not, be fully relied on, I fhall only make a medical remark or two. Notwithftanding Mr. Howard's conviction of having caught the contagion from the young lady, I think the diftance of time between his laft vifit to her and his own feizure, makes the fact dubious. Contagion thus fenfibly received, ufually, I believe, operates in a lefs period than

* *This muft probably have been only fome directions to his executors, as his will is dated in 17*7.

L 2

five days*. Perhaps his vifit to the hofpitals on the 6th, or his late return from the Admiral's on the 8th, in a cold feafon and unwholefome climate, will better account for it. The nature of his complaint is not very clear, for it is very uncommon for the fenfes to remain entire till the laft, in a fever of the low or putrid kind ; nor are fits, refembling epileptic attacks, among the ufual fymptoms of fuch a difeafe. That a wandering gout might make part of his indifpofition, is not very improbable, as it was a diforder to which he was conftitutionally liable, though his mode of living prevented any fevere paroxyfms of it. At any rate, his difeafe was certainly attended with debility of the vital powers, and therefore the long and frequent ufe of James' powders muft have been prejudicial. And I think it highly probable, that Mr. Howard's name may be added to the numerous lift of thofe, whofe lives have been facrificed to the empirical ufe of a medicine of great activity, and therefore capable of doing much harm as well as good.

---

* *According to Dr. Lind, its effects, fhivering and ficknefs, are inftantaneous. See Differt. on Fevers and Infection. Chap. ii. fect. 1.*

It was Mr. Howard's written requeſt, that his papers ſhould be correɛted and fitted for publication by Dr. Price and myſelf. The declining ſtate of health of Dr. Price*, has

* *Whilſt I am engaged in this work, Dr. Price has followed his friend to the grave. A charaɛter ſo illuſtrious will, doubtleſs, have all juſtice done it by ſome pen qualified to diſplay its various merits. May I be permitted, however, to take this occaſion of mingling my regrets with thoſe of his other friends and admirers, and offering a ſmall tribute to the memory of one of the moſt excellent of men! Though during life the advanced ſtation he occupied in political controverſy rendered his name as obnoxious to ſome, as it was cheriſhed and revered by others, yet now he is gone to that place where all worldly differences are at an end, it may be hoped, that the liberal of all denominations will concur, in reſpeɛting a long courſe of years ſpent in the unremitted application of eminent abilities and acquirements, to the promotion of what he regarded as the greateſt good of his fellow-creatures. A charaɛter in which were combined ſimplicity of heart, with depth of underſtanding,—ardent love of truth, with true Chriſtian charity and humility;—high zeal for the public intereſts, with perfeɛt freedom from all private views; cannot be ultimately injured by the petulence of wit, or the inveɛtives of eloquence. Dr. Price's reputation as a moraliſt, philoſopher, and politician, may ſafely be committed to impartial poſterity.*

caufed the bufinefs to devolve folely on me,
and I have executed it to the beft of my power. Little was requifite to be done to the
greateft part, which he had himfelf copied out
fair. The reft was with fome difficulty to be
compiled out of detached and broken memorandums; but in thefe his own words are as
much as poffible preferved. Of this Supple-
ment I fhall give a general account, as I have
done of the former parts of his works.

The order and regularity of Holland ftill
afford ufeful defcriptions, and fome of the a-
bufes which even there had crept in, feem to
have been corrected fince Mr. Howard's vifits.
The friend to humanity has yet, however, to
lament the continued ufe of the torture there,
to force confeffion. The ftate of the prifons in
Ofnaburgh, Hanover, and Brunfwick, is again
dwelt upon with fome minutenefs, obvioufly
becaufe the writer thought there was fome
probability of his attracting, in a more peculiar
manner, the notice of thofe who have the
power of remedying their defects. Who will
not fympathize with him in the difappointment
he expreffes in this inftance, and bewail the
ftrange fatality by which the utmoft barbarity
of the torture is retained in the dominions of a

mild and enlightened Sovereign, whofe inter-
pofitions could not but be efficacious in fuppref-
fing it !

At Berlin and Spandau the inftitutions appear to preferve the good order in which they
were left by the Great Frederic. Konigfberg
feéms to fhew the neglect incident to places diftant from the feat of government. In a note
under this place, Mr. Howard makes an acknowledgment of the attention with which his
remarks have been honored in various foreign
countries, and properly adduces it as a reafon
for his adoption of that cenforial manner of
noting abufes, which, in his later journies, he
has not fcrupled freely to employ.

At St. Peterfburgh he had the pleafure to
obferve feveral improvements in the hofpitals,
probably in great part owing to his own fuggeftions. Under Cronftadt he finds occafion,
however, to animadvert upon an alteration in
the plan of diet, generally adopted throughout
the marine and military hofpitals of Ruffia,
which, in his opinion, is highly prejudicial.
This alteration confifts in changing milk, and
various other articles, conftituting the ufual li-
quid and middle diet of the fick, for the ftrong-

er and lefs digeftible food of men in health. The prifons at Mofcow feem greatly neglected by thofe whofe office it is to fuperintend them ; but the charity difplayed by individuals towards the poor wretches confined in them, gave Mr. Howard a favorable idea of the humane difpofition of the nation, confirmed by what he faw of their manners in his travels.

He now haftened to thofe fcenes, where a deftructive war, co-operating with an unwholefome climate, produced fuch evils, aggravated by neglect and inhumanity, that they gave him no other occupation than to lament and complain. After all the allowances that candor demands, for inevitable wants and hardfhips in the diftant pofts of a newly poffcffed country, and during the heighth of widely extended military operations, the Ruffian commanders cannot be vindicated from an inattention to the lives and comforts of their foldiers, greater, as Mr. Howard obferves, than he had fcen in any other country. Ignorance, abufe, mifmanagement, and deficiency, feem at their very fummit in the military hofpitals of Cherfon, Witowka, and St. Nicholas. The lively pictures he has drawn of the diftreffes he here witneffed, and his pathetic defcription of the fufferings of the poor recruits, marched from their diftant homes to thefe melancholy regions, muft awaken in every feeling breaft a warm indignation againft the fchemes of ambitious defpotifm, however varnifhed over with the coloring of glory, or even of national utility. No leffon ought to be more forcibly impreffed on mankind, than, that uncontroled power in one or few, notwithftanding it may occafionally be exercifed in fplendid and even beneficent defigns, is on the whole abfolutely inconfiftent with the happinefs of a people*. The Emprefs of Ruffia's unjuft feizure of Leffer and Crim Tartary, has been the caufe of miferies not to be calculated, to her own fubjects and thofe of Turkey, and has endangered the tranquility of all Europe.

I fhall conclude this review of the works and public fervices of Mr. Howard with brief annals of his more than Herculean labors, during the laft feventeen years of his life.

---

* Scilicet ut Turno contingat regia conjunx
Nos, animæ viles, inhumata infletaque turba,
Sternamur campis.   Æn. xi.

1773. High-fheriff of Bedfordfhire. Vifited many county and town gaols.

1774. Completed his furvey of Englifh
gaols. Stood candidate to reprefent
the town of Bedford.

1775. Travelled to Scotland, Ireland,
France, Holland, Flanders and Germany.

1776. Repeated his vifit to the above countries, and to Switzerland. During
thefe two years revifited all the Englifh gaols.

1777. Printed his ftate of prifons.

1778. Travelled through Holland, Flanders,
Germany, Italy, Switzerland, and
part of France.

1779. Revifited all the counties of England
and Wales, and travelled into Scotland and Ireland. Acted as Supervi-
for of the Penitentiary Houfes.

1780. Printed his firft Apendix.

1781. Travelled into Denmark, Sweden, Ruſſia, Poland, Germany, and Holland.

1782. Again ſurveyed all the Engliſh priſons, and went into Scotland and Ireland.

1783. Viſited Portugal, Spain, France, Flanders and Holland : alſo, Scotland and Ireland ; and viewed ſeveral Engliſh priſons.

1784. Printed the ſecond Appendix, and a new edition of his whole works.

1785.
1786.
1787. ⎰ From the cloſe of the firſt of theſe years, to the beginning of the laſt, on his tour through Holland, France, Italy, Malta, Turkey and Germany. Afterwards went to Scotland and Ireland.

1788. Reviſited Ireland; and during this and the former year, travelled over all England.

1789. Printed his work on Lazarettos, &c.
Travelled through Holland, Germany, Pruffia, and Livenia, to Ruffia
and Leffer Tartary.

-

1790. January 20. Died at Cherfon.

Having thus traced the footfteps of this great
philanthropift from the cradle to the grave, and
followed them with clofe infpection in that part
of his courfe which comprehends his more
public life, it only remains, to affemble thofe
features of character which have been difplayed in his actions, and to form them in conjunction with fuch minuter ftrokes as ftudious obfervation may have enabled me to draw, into a
faithful portraiture of the man.

The firft thing that ftruck an obferver on
acquaintance with Mr. Howard, was a ftamp
of extraordinary vigour and energy on all his
movements and expreffions. An eye lively and
penetrating, ftrong and prominant features,
quick gait, and animated geftures, gave pro-
mife of ardor in forming, and vivacity in exe-

cuting his defigns*. At no time of his life, I believe, was he without fome object of warm purfuit; and in every thing he purfued, he was indefatigable in aiming at perfection. Give him a hint of any thing he had left fhoit, or any new acquifition to be made, and while you might fuppofe he was deliberating about it, you were furprifed with finding it was done. Not Cæfar himfelf could better exemplify the poet's

Nil actum credens, dum quid fapereffet agendum.

I remember that, having accidentally remarked to him that amongft the London prifons he

---

* *Mr. Howard had fo much contempt for worldly honors that he would never fit to any painter whatever, and this has given rife to an opinion that there is no correct likenefs of him. In this refpect, however, the public feem to be under a miftake. An ingenious and refpectable artift, Mr. T. Holloway, whofe talents are juftly admired, had often an opportunity of being in company with Mr. Howard in a public place, where a fketch of his features might be ftolen. The temptation was too great to be refifted. An accurate fketch was made, and an engraving, executed from it, accompanies this life, and will afford a very juft idea of the features of this great and good man.*

. The American Editor can affure the public, that, the original fketch alluded to above, is now in the poffeffion of Mr. Caleb Lownes of this city.

had omitted the Tower, he was so struck with the deficiency (though of trifling consequence, since confinement there is so rare), that at his very first leisure he ran to London, and supplied it. Nor was it only during a short period of ardour that his exertions were thus awakened. He had the still rarer quality of being able, for any length of time, to bend all the powers and faculties of his mind to one point, unseduced by every allurement which curiosity or any other affection might throw in his way, and unsusceptible of that satiety and disgust which are so apt to steal upon a protracted pursuit. Though by his early travels he had shewn himself not indifferent to those objects of taste and information which strike the cultivated mind in a foreign country, yet in the tours expressly made for the purpose of examining prisons and hospitals, he appears to have had eyes and ears for nothing else: at least he suffered no other object to detain him or draw him aside*. Impressed with the idea of the importance of his designs, and the uncertainty of human life, he was impatient to get as much done

---

* *He mentioned being once prevailed upon in Italy, to go and hear some extraordinary fine music ; but, finding his thoughts too much occupied by it, he would never repeat the indulgence.*

as poffible within the allotted limits. And in
this difpolition confifted that enthufiafm by
which the public fuppofed him actuated; for
otherwife, his cool and fteady temper gave no
idea of the character ufually diftinguifhed by
that appellation. He followed his plans, indeed,
with wonderful vigour and conftancy, but by
no means with that heat and eagernefs, that in-
flamed and exalted imagination, which de-
note the enthufiaft. Hence, he was not liable
to catch at partial reprefentations, to view
facts through fallacious mediums, and to fall
into thofe miftakes which are fo frequent in
the refearches of the man of fancy and warm
feeling. Some perfons, who only knew him
by his extraordinary actions, were ready e-
nough to beftow upon him that fneer of contempt, which men of cold hearts and felfifh
difpofitions are fo apt to apply to whatever has
the fhew of high fenfibility. While others,
who had a flight acquaintance with him, and
faw occafional features of phlegm, and perhaps
harfhnefs, were difpofed to queftion his feeling
altogether, and to attribute his exertions either merely to a fenfe of duty, or to habit
and humour. But both thefe were erroneous
conclufions. He felt as a man fhould feel; but
not fo as to miflead him, either in the eftimate

he formed of objects of utility, or in his rea-
fonings concerning the means by which they
were to be brought into effect. The reformation of abufes, and the relief of mifery, were
the two great purpofes which he kept in view
in all his undertakings; and I have equally
feen the tear of fenfibility ftart into his eyes
on recalling fome of the diftrefsful fcenes to
which he had been witnefs, and the fpirit of
indignation flafh from them on relating inftances of bafenefs and oppreffion. Still, however,
his conftancy of mind and felf-collection never
deferted him. He was never agitated, never
off his guard; and the unfpeakable advantages of fuch a temper in the fcenes in which he
was engaged, need not be dwelt upon.

His whole courfe of action was fuch a trial
of intrepidity and fortitude, that it may feem
altogether fuperfluous to fpeak of his poffeffion
of thefe qualities. He had them, indeed, both
from nature and principle. His nerves were
firm; and his conviction of marching in the
path of duty made him fearlefs of confequences. Nor was it only on great occafions that
this ftrength of mind was fhown. It raifed
him above falfe fhame, and that awe which
makes a coward of many a brave man in the

prefence of a fuperior. No one ever lefs "feared the face of man," than he. No one hefitated lefs in fpeaking bold truths, or a-vowing obnoxious opinions. His courage was equally paffive and active. He was prepared to make every facrifice that a regard to ftrict veracity, or rigorous duty, could enjoin; and it cannot be doubted, that, had he lived in an age when afferting his civil and religious rights would have fubjected him to martyrdom, not a more willing martyr would ever have afcended the fcaffold, or embraced the ftake.

The refolute temper of Mr. Howard dif-played itfelf in a certain peremptorinefs, which, when he had once determined, rendered him unyielding to perfuafion or diffaufion, and urg-ed him on to the accomplifhment of his pur-pofe, regardlefs of obftacles. He expected prompt obedience in thofe from whom he had a right to require it, and was not a man to be treated with negligence and inattention. He was, however, extremely confiderate, and fuf-ficiently indulgent to human frailties; and a good-will to pleafe him could fcarcely fail of its effect. That his commands were reafona-ble, and his expectations moderate, may be in-ferred from the long continuance of moft of

his fervants with him, and his fteady attachment to many of thofe whom he employed.
His means of enforcing compliance were chiefly
rewards; and the withholding them was his
method of fhowing difpleafure*.

* *The following characterific anecdote was communicated to me by a gentleman who travelled in a
chaife with him from Lancafhire to London in 1777.
Mr. Howard obferved, that he had found few things
more difficult to manage than poft-chaife drivers, who
would feldom comply with his wifhes of going flow or
faft, till he adopted the following method. At the end
of a ftage, when the driver had been perverfe, he de-.
fired the landlord to fend for fome poor induftrious widow, or other proper objeêt of charity, and to introduce fuch perfon and the driver together. He then paid
the latter his fare, and told him, that as he had not
thought proper to attend to his repeated requefts as to
the manner of being driven, he fhould not make him
any prefent; but, to fhow him that he did not withhold
it out of a principle of parfimony, he would give the
poor perfon prefent double the fum ufually given to a
poftillion. This he did, and difmiffed the parties. He
had not long practifed this mode, he faid, before he
experienced the good effects of it on all the roads where
he was known.*

*A more extraordinary inftance of his determined fpi-
rit has been related to me. Travelling once in the king*

The spirit of independence by which he was ever distinguished, had in him the only foundation to be relied on, moderate desires. Perfectly contented with the competence which Providence had bestowed on him, he never had a thought of increasing it; and even when in a situation to expect a family, he made it a rule with himself to lay up no part of his annual income, but to expend in some useful or benevolent scheme the superfluity of the year.

of Pruffia's dominions, he came to a very narrow piece of road, admitting only one carriage, where it was enjoined on all postillions entering at each end, to blow their horns by way of notice. His did so; but, after proceeding a good way, they met a courier travelling on the king's business, who had neglected this precaution. The courier ordered Mr. Howard's postillion to turn back; but Mr. Howard remonstrated, that he had complied with the rule, while the other had violated it; and therefore that he should insist on going forwards. The courier, relying on an authority, to which, in that country, every thing must give way, made use of high words, but in vain. As neither was disposed to yield, they sat still a long time in their respective carriages: at length the courier gave up the point to the sturdy Englishman, who would on no account renounce his rights.

Left this fhould be converted into a charge of careleffnefs in providing for his own, it may be proper to mention, that he had the beft-grounded expectations, that any children he might have, would largely partake of the wealth of their relations. Thus he preferved his heart from that contamination, which (taking in the whole of life) is perhaps the difeafe moft frequently attendant on a ftate of profperity,—the luft of growing rich ; a paffion, which is too often found to fwallow up liberality, public fpirit, and, at laft, that independency, which it is the beft ufe of wealth to fecure. By this temper of mind he was elevated to an immeafurable diftance above every thing mean and fordid ; and in all his tranfactions he difplayed a fpirit of honor and generofity, that might become the "blood of the Howards" when flowing in its nobleft channels.

Had Mr. Howard been lefs provided with the goods of fortune, his independency would have found a refource in the fewnefs of his wants; and it was an ineftimable advantage which he brought to his great work, an advantage perhaps more uncommon in this country than any of thofe already mentioned, that he poffeffed a command over all corporeal ap-

petites and habitudes, not lefs perfect than that
of any ancient philofopher, or modern afcetic.
The ftrict regimen of diet which he had adopted early in life from motives of health, he afterwards perfevered in through choice, and
even extended its rigour, fo as to reject all
thofe indulgencies which even the moft tempe-
rate confider as neceffary for the prefervation
of their ftrength and vigor. Animal foods,
and fermented and fpirituous drinks, he utter-
ly difcarded from his diet. Water and the
plaineft vegetables fufficed him. Milk, tea,
butter, and fruit, were his luxuries; and he
was equally fparing in the quantity of food,
and indifferent as to the ftated times of taking
it. Thus he found his wants fupplied in almoft every place where man exifted, and was
as well provided in the pofadas of Spain and
caravanferas of Turkey, as in the inns and
hotels of England and France. Water was
one of his principal neceffaries, for he was a
very Muffelman in his ablutions; and if nicety
or delicacy had place with him in any refpect,
it was in the perfect cleanlinefs of his whole
perfon. He was equally tolerant of heat, cold,
and all the viciffitudes of climate; and, what
is more wonderful, not even fleep feemed neceffary to him, at leaft at thofe returns and in

thofe proportions in which mankind in genera l expect it. How well he was capable of enduring fatigue, the amazing journies he took by all modes of conveyance, without any inter-vals of what might be called repofe (fince his only baiting places were his proper fcenes of action), abundantly teftify. In fhort no human body was probably ever more perfectly the fervant of the mind by which it was actuated; and all the efforts of the ftrongeft conftitution, not inured to habits of felf-denial, and moral as well as corporeal exercife, would have been unequal to his exertions*.

With refpect to the character of his under-ftanding, that, too, was as happily adapted to the great bufinefs in which ne engaged.

* *The following account of his mode of travelling, communicated to me by a gentleman in Dublin, who had much free converfation with him, and the fubftance of which I well recollect to have heard from himfelf, will, I doubt not, prove interefting. " When he travelled in England or Ireland, it was generally on horfeback, and he rode about forty Englifh miles a day. He was never at a lofs for an inn. When in Ireland, or the Highlands of Scotland, he ufed to ftop at one of the poor cabins that ftick up a rag by way of fign, and get a little milk.*

He had not, in a high degree, that extensive comprehension, that faculty of generalizing, which is said to distinguish the man of genius, but which, without a previous collection of authentic materials, is ever apt to lead into erroneous speculations. He was rather a man of

When he came to the town he was to sleep at, he bespoke a supper, with wine and beer, like another traveller, but made his man attend him, and take it away, whilst he was preparing his bread and milk. He always paid the waiters, postillions, &c. liberally, because he would have no discontent or dispute, nor suffer his spirits to be agitated for such a matter; saying, that in a journey that might cost three or four hundred pounds, fifteen or twenty pounds addition was not worth thinking about. When he travelled on the continent, he usually went post in his own chaise, which was a German one that he bought for the purpose. He never stopped till he came to the town he meant to visit, but travelled all night, if necessary; and from habit could sleep very well in the chaise for several nights together. In the last tour but one he travelled twenty days and nights together without going to bed, and found no inconvenience from it. He used to carry with him a small tea-kettle, some cups, a little pot of sweetmeats, and a few loaves. At the post-house he could get his water boiled, send out for milk, and make his repast, while his man went to the auberge.'*

N

detail; of laborious accuracy and minute examination; and therefore he had the proper
qualities for one who was to lead the way in
refearches where all was ignorance, confufion,
and local cuftom. Who but fuch a man could
have collected a body of information, which
has made even profeffional men acquainted with
interefting facts that they never before knew;
and has given the Englifh reader a more exact
knowledge of practices followed in Ruffia and
Spain, than he before had of thofe in his own
country? This minutenefs of detail was what
he ever regarded as his peculiar province. As
he was of all men the moft modeft eftimator of
his own abilities, he was ufed to fay, "I am
the *plodder*, who goes about to collect materials
for men of genius to make ufe of." Let thofe
who look with faftidioufnefs upon long tables
of rules and orders, and meafurements of cells
and work-rooms, given in feet and inches,
confider, that when a fcheme is brought into
practice, thefe fmall circumftances muft have
their place; and that the moft ingenious plans
often fail in their execution for want of adjuft-
ment in the nicer parts. Perhaps even the
great Frederic of Pruffia was more indebted
for fuccefs to the exactnefs of his difpofitions in
every minute particular connected with prac-

tice, than to deep and fublime views of general principles.

From a fimilar caft of mind, Mr. Howard
was a friend to fubordination, and all the de-
corums of regular fociety ; nor did he diflike
vigorous exertions of civil authority, when directed to laudable purpofes. He interfered
little in difputes relative to the theory of government; but was contented to take fyftems
of fovereignty as he found them eftablifhed in
various parts of the world, fatisfied with
prompting fuch an application of their powers
as might promote the welfare of the refpective
communities. A ftate of imprifonment being
that in which the rights of men are, in great
part, at leaft, fufpended, it was natural that
his thoughts fhould be more converfant with a
people as the fubjects, than as the fource, of
authority. Yet he well knew, and properly
valued, the ineftimable bleffings of political
freedom, as oppofed to defpotifm ; and, among
the nations of Europe, he confidered the Dutch
and Swifs as affording the beft examples of a
ftrict and fteady police, conducted upon principles of equity and humanity. To the character of the Dutch he was, indeed, peculiarly,
partial ; and frequently afferted, that he fhould

prefer Holland for his place of refidence, to any other foreign country. I can add, from undoubted authority, that Mr. Howard was one of thofe who (in the language of the great Lord Chatham) " rejoiced that America had refifted," and triumphed in her final fuccefs; and that he was principally attached to the popular part of our conftitution; and that in his own county he diftinguifhed himfelf by a fpirited oppofition to ariftocratical influence.

His peculiar habits of life, and the exclufive attention he beftowed in his later years on a few objects, caufed him to appear more averfe to fociety than I think he really was; and it has been mentioned as an unfortunate circumftance, that his fhynefs and referve frequently kept him out of the way of perfons from whom he might have derived much ufeful information. But it is vain to defire things incompatible. Mr. Howard can fcarcely be denied to have chofen the beft way, upon the whole, of conducting his enquiries; and if he had been a a more *companionable* man, more ready to indulge his own curiofity, and gratify that of others, he would no longer have poffeffed one of the chief advantages he brought to his great work. Yet while he affiduoufly fhunned all engagements which would have involved him in the forms and diffipation of fociety, he was by no means difinclined to enter into converfations on his particular topics ; on the contrary, he was often extremely communicative, and would enliven a fmall circle with the moft entertaining relations of his travels and adventures.

Mr. Howard had in a high degree that refpectful attention to the female fex which fo much characterifes the gentleman. Perhaps, indeed, I may here be referring to rules of politenefs which no longer exift. But he was as thoroughly impreffed with the maxim of *place aux dames* as any Frenchman, though without the ftrain of light and complimentary gallantry which has accompanied it in the individuals of that nation. His was a more ferious fentiment, connected with the uniform practice of giving up his own eafe and accommodation, for the fake of doing a real kindnefs to any female of decent character. It is excellently illuftrated by an anecdote related in a magazine, by a perfon who chanced to fail with him in the packet from Holyhead to Dublin, when the veffel being much crowded, Mr. Howard refigned his bed to a fervant-maid, and took up with the cabin floor for himself. It is likewise displayed throughout his works, by the warmth with which he always censures the practice of putting female prisoners in irons, and exposing them to any harsh and indelicate treatment. He was fond of nothing so much as the conversation of women of education and cultivated manners, and studied to attach them by little elegant presents, and other marks of attention. Indeed, his soft tone of voice and gentleness of demeanour might be thought to approach somewhat to the effeminate, and would surprise those who had known him only by the energy of his exertions. In his judgment of female character, it was manifest that the idea of his lost Harriet was the standard of excellence; and, if ever he had married again, a resemblance to her would have been the principal motive of his choice. I recollect to this purpose a singular anecdote, which he related to us on his return from one of his tours. In going from one town in Holland to another in the common passage boat, he was placed near an elderly gentleman, who had in company a young lady of a most engaging manner and appearance, which very strongly reminded him of his Harriet. He was so much struck with her, that, on arriving at the place of deſtination, he cauſed his ſervant to follow them, and get intelligence who they were. It was not without ſome diſappointment that he learned, that the old gentleman was an eminent merchant, and the young lady,—*his wiſe*.

Mr. Howard's predilection for female ſociety, was in part a conſequence of his abhorrence of every thing groſs and licentious. His own language and manners were invariably pure and delicate ; and the freedoms which paſs uncenſured or even applauded in the promiſcuous companies of men, would have affected him with ſenſations of diſguſt. For a perſon poſſeſſed of ſuch feelings, to have brought himſelf to ſubmit to ſuch frequent communication with the moſt abandoned of mankind, was perhaps a greater triumph of duty over inclination than any other he obtained in the proſecution of his deſigns. Yet the nature of his errand to priſons probably inſpired awe and reſpect in the moſt diſſolute ; and I think he has recorded, that he never met with a ſingle inſult from the priſoners in any of the gaols he viſited.

As Mr. Howard was ſo eminently a religious character, it may be expected that ſomewhat more ſhould be ſaid of the peculiar tenets he adopted. But, besides that this was a topic which did not enter into our conversations, I confess, I do not perceive how his general plan of conduct was likely to be influenced by any peculiarity of that kind. The principle of religious duty, which is nearly the same in all systems, and differs rather in strength than in kind in different persons, is surely sufficient to account for all that he did and underwent in promoting the good of mankind, by modes which Providence seemed to place before him. It has been suggested, that he was much under the influence of the doctrine of predestination; and I know not what of sternness has been attributed to him as its natural consequence. For my own part, I am not able to discover in what those notions of Providence, general and particular, which make part of the profession of all religions, differ essentially from the opinions of the predestinarians; and, from manifold observation, I am certain, that the reception of the doctrine of predestination, as an article of belief, does not necessarily imply those practical consequences which might seem deducible from it. The language, at least, of our lower classes of people is almost universally founded upon it; but when one them dies of an infectious disease, notwithstanding the byſtanders all ſpeak of the event as fated and inevitable, yet each, for himſelf, does not the leſs avoid the infection, or the leſs recur to medical aid if attacked by it. With reſpect to Mr. Howard, he never ſeemed to adopt the idea that he was moved by an irreſiſtible impulſe to his deſigns; for they were the ſubject of much thought and diſcuſſion: nor did he confront dangers becauſe he had a perſuaſion that he ſhould be preſerved from their natural conſequences, but becauſe he was elevated above them. This ſentiment he has himſelf more than once expreſſed in print; and ſurely none could be either more rational, or more adequate to the effects produced. " Being in the way of my duty (ſays he), I fear no evil." I may venture to affirm, that thoſe of the medical profeſſion, whoſe fearleſſneſs is not merely the reſult of habit, muſt reaſon upon the ſame principle, when they calmly expoſe themſelves to ſimilar hazards. They, for the moſt part, uſe no precautions againſt contagion: Mr. Howard did uſe ſome; though their effects were probably trifling compared with that of his habitual temperance and cleanlineſs, and his untroubled ſerenity of mind. On the whole, his religious confidence does not appear to have been of a nature different from that of other pious men; but to be fo fteadily and uniformly under its influence, and to be elevated by it to fuch a fuperiority to all worldly confiderations, can be the lot of none but thofe who have formed early habits of referring every thing to the divine will, and of fixing all their views on futurity.

From Mr. Howard's connexions with thofe fects who have ever fhewn a particular abhorrence of the frauds and fuperftitions of popery, it might be fuppofed, that he would look with a prejudiced eye on the profeffors and minifters of that perfuafion. But fuch was his veneration for true vital religion, that he was as ready to pay it honour when he met with it in the habit of a monk, as, under the garb of a teacher: and throughout his works, as well as in converfation, he ever dwelt with great complacency on the pure zeal for the good of mankind, and genuine Chriftian charity, which he frequently difcovered among the Roman Catholic clergy, both regular and fecular. He was no friend to that hafty diffolution of convents and monaftaries which formed part of the multifarious reforms of the late Emperor of Germany. He pitied the aged inmates, male and female, of thefe quiet

abodes, who were driven from their beloved
retreats into the wide world, with a very
flender and often ill-paid pittance for their
fupport. " Why might not they (he would
fay) be fuffered gradually to die away, and be
tranfplanted from one religious houfe to another as their numbers leffened ?" Thofe orders which make it the great duty of their
profeffion to attend with the kindeft affiduity
upon the fick and imprifoned, and who therefore came continually within his notice, feemed to conciliate his good will to the whole
fraternity; and the virtues of order, decency,
fobriety, and charity, fo much akin to his own,
naturally inclined him to a kind of fellowfhip
with them. He rigoroufly, however, abftained
from any compliances with their worfhip which
he thought unlawful ; and gave them his efteem as men, without the leaft difpofition to
concur with them as theologians.

Such were the great lines of Mr. Howard's
character—lines ftrongly marked, and fufficient
to difcriminate him from any of thofe who
have appeared in a part fomewhat fimilar to
his own on the theatre of the world. The
union of qualities which fo peculiarly fitted
him for the poft he undertook, is not likely, in

our age, again to take place; yet different combinations may be employed to effect the same purposes; and, with respect to the objects of police and humanity concerning which he occupied himself, the information he has ollected will render the repetition of labours like his unnecessary. To propose as a model, a character marked with such singularities, and, no doubt, with some foibles, would be equally vain and injudicious; but his firm attachment to principle, high sense of honor, pure benevolence, unshaken constancy, and indefatigable perseverance, may properly be held up to the view of all persons occupying important stations, or engaged in useful enterprises, as qualities not less to be imitated, than admired.

I shall conclude with some account of the *literary honors* which Mr. Howard has received from his countrymen. It would, indeed, have been extraordinary, if, while senates and courts of judicature offered him their tribute of applause, poetry and eloquence should have shewn an infensibility to his merits. Besides the acknowledgments paid him in every publication upon topics similar to his own, he became the theme of the elegant muse of Mr. Hayley, who addressed to him an ode in the year 1780, to which reference has already been made. That celebrated poem is, by the American Editor, fubjoined to the prefent work. In the fucceeding year, Mr. Burke, adverting, in a fpeech to the Freemen of Briftol, to a fact in Mr. Howard's book, ftruck out, with the enthufiafm of genius, into a panegyrical digreffion on his plans and actions, decorated with his peculiar ftrain of glowing imagery. Nothing, perhaps, can more forcibly exprefs the general idea entertained of Mr. Howard's exalted worth than the following extract from that fpeech. " I cannot name this gentleman, fays " Mr. Burke, I cannot name this gentleman, " without remarking that his labours and wri- " tings have done much to open the eyes and " hearts of mankind. He has vifited *all Eu-* " *rope*, not to furvey the fumptuoufnefs of pa- " laces, nor the ftatelinefs of temples; not to " make accurate meafurements of the remains " of ancient grandeur, nor to form a fcale of " the curiofities of modern art; not to collect " medals, nor to collate manufcripts; but to " dive into the depths of dungeons, to plunge " into the infection of hofpitals; to furvey the " manfions of forrow and pain; to take guage " and dimenfions of mifery, depreffion, and " contempt; to remember the forgotten; to

O

" attend to the neglected; to visit the forsak-
" en; and to compare and collate the distresses
" of all men in all countries. His plan is ori-
" ginal, and it is as full of genius, as it is of
" humanity. It is a voyage of *philanthropy*
" —a circumnavigation of *charity!* Already
" the benefit of this labor itself is felt more or
" less in every country: I hope he will anti-
" cipate his final reward by seeing all its effects
" fully realized in his own. He will receive,
" not in retail but in grofs, the reward of those
" who visit the prisoner, and he has so far
" forestalled and monopolised this branch of
" charity, that there will be, I trust, little
" room to merit by such acts of benevolence
" hereafter." This speech was afterwards
printed, and the passage concerning Mr. Howard was copied into various periodical writings,
and read with universal approbation. His
character was even exhibited on the stage; for
a comedy of Mrs. Inchbald's, entitled Such
Things Are, contained a part evidently modelled upon his peculiar cast of benevolence,
which for a time rendered the piece popular.

Dr. Darwin's very beautiful poem of *the
Botanic Garden*, printed in 1789, amidst an un-

expected variety of subjects, presents an eulogium of Mr. Howard, so appropriate and poetical, that I am sure no reader of taste will require an apology from me for inserting it.

—And now BENEVOLENCE! thy rays divine
Dart round the globe from Zembla to the Line:
O'er each dark prison plays the cheering light,
Like northern lustres o'er the vault of night.—
From realm to realm, with cross or crescent crown'd,
Where'er mankind and misery are found,
O'er burning sands, deep waves, or wilds of snow,
Thy HOWARD journeying seeks the house of woe.
Down many a winding step to dungeons dank,
Where anguish wails aloud, and fetters clank;
To caves bestrew'd with many a mouldering bone,
And cells, whose echoes only learn to groan;
Where no kind bars a whispering friend disclose,
No sunbeam enters, and no zephyr blows,
He treads, inemulous of fame or wealth,
Profuse of toil, and prodigal of health;
With soft assuasive eloquence expands
Power's rigid heart, and opes his clenching hands;
Leads stern-ey'd justice to the dark domains,
If not to sever, to relax the chains;
Or guides awaken'd mercy through the gloom,
And shews the prison, sister to the tomb!—
Gives to her babes the self-devoted wife,
To her fond husband liberty and life!—
—The spirits of the good, who bend from high

Wide o'er thefe earthly fcenes their partial eye,.
When firft, array'd in VIRTUE's pureft robe,
They faw her HOWARD traverfing the globe ;
Saw round his brows her fun-like glory blaze
In arrowy circles of unwearied rays ;
Miftook a mortal for an angel-gueft,
And afk'd what feraph-foot the earth impreft.
—Onward he moves '—Difeafe and death retire,
And murmuring demons hate him, and admire.

After thefe lines, the Editor avails himfelf
of this favorable opportunity of exhibiting to
the public, an extract from the funeral fermon
occafioned by the death of Mr. Howard. And
as it was delivered under the influence of heart-
felt emotions, accompanied with ferious regret,
and refers to the leading principle of all his
actions, it is prefumed, that it will not be
deemed mifplaced, at the clofe of a volume,
the purpofe of which is, to reprefent in ftrong,.
faithful, and glowing colours the character of
the BENEVOLENT HOWARD.

" Thofe who beft knew Mr. Howard," fays
Mr. Palmer*, in his fermon on the death of
his benevolent friend, " are fo well acquainted

* *Reverend Mr. Palmer of Hackney.*

with the ftrength of his Chriftian principles, and with his evangelical views, as not to en-tertain a doubt but that, during his laft ficknefs and in the profpect of death, (melancholy as his fituation was, at a diftance from all his friends) he exercifed the greateft degree of firmnefs, patience, and fubmiffion to the Divine will ; a lively faith in the promifes of the gof-pel; a cheerful confidence in the grace of God, in a Redeemer, for accceptance, renouncing, as he often had explicitly done, all pretenfions to merit by all the good works he had perform-ed ; and an humble triumph in the profpect of life eternal, as the free gift of God through Jefus Chrift. A little before he left England, when a friend expreffed his concern at parting with him, from an apprehenfion that they fhould never meet again, he cheerfully replied, " We fhall foon meet in Heaven ;" and, as he rather expected to die of the plague in Egypt, he added, "the way to Heaven from Grand Cairo is as near as from London." He that thus lived in the hope of immortality, may well be fuppofed at death to have experienced a joy unfpeakable and full of glory."

nature and of the religion of Jefus. As his
life was fingularly ufeful, his death was equally
glorious. He fell a martyr in the caufe of humanity. As thoufands bleffed him while living,
millions will lament him now dead. A greater lofs this country, may I not fay this world,
has feldom fuftained. It may appear to many
a myfterious providence, that fuch a friend to
his fpecies fhould be cut off at a time when he
had fuch noble ends in view, and when, confidering the vigour of his conftitution at the age
of fixty-five, he might have been expected to
continue fome years as a bleffing to his native
country, particularly in promoting the execution of the plans which he had fuggefted in his
publications. But his work was done : the defigns of Providence by him were accomplifhed ;
and doubtlefs all the circumftances of his death
were wifely ordered by Him who doth all
things well, and who can eafily raife up other
inftruments for perfecting what he had begun."

" His being cut off in a foreign country, however grievous it may be to his friends here, is a
circumftance, which may probably be wifely
defigned, and happily over-ruled, for fome
very important purpofes in that rifing kingdom,
which will efteem itfelf honoured by entombing

fuch a patriotic Englifhman; and where a fpirit of emulation may probably be excited to
imitate his virtues, and to adopt his plans, for
promoting the growing glory and happinefs of
that vaft empire."

"While therefore we devoutly praife God
for what he had done by this his eminent fervant, let us fubmit to his will, and adore his
wifdom and fovereignty in his removal. And
let us make the beft improvement of fo affecting
a difpenfation; particularly by cultivating that
benevolence by which the deceafed was actuated, and by doing what we can, in our different
fpheres, for repairing his lofs. This will be
the beft way of expreffing our veneration for
his character, and doing honour to his memory."

"That others, upon his deceafe, would be
excited to profecute fome of his fchemes for
the public good, he himfelf had a firm perfuafion. This made him the lefs anxious about his
own life, which his friends thought of fo much
importance. In the laft converfation I had
with him, when I expreffed my fears for his
fafety, and my wifhes that he could have been
prevailed upon to continue at home, in order

to carry into execution the generous plans he had formed for the good of his country, his anſwer was, "When I am dead ſome body elſe will take up the matter and carry it through." God grant that his expectations may be veriſied!—But where is the man to be found who is like-minded with him? Another HOWARD this country cannot hope to ſee. Nor is one, altogether his equal now needed. He laid a foundation, on which it would be comparatively eaſy to build. He, with incredible labour and expence, has broken up the ground, prepared the ſoil, and ſown the ſeed: to raiſe and gather the crop will require but a ſmall portion of induſtry and public ſpirit. And are there none among you, ye men of fortune and leiſure, in whom that portion of induſtry and public ſpirit is to be found? Ye who, in the ſtrongeſt terms language can ſupply, celebrate the philanthropy of the deceaſed, and have ſhewn yourſelves impatient to erect a monument to his honor, ſo as ſcarcely to be reſtrained from hurting his modeſty while yet alive; is there no one among you that wiſhes to inherit his virtues, and rear the glorious fabric he had framed? Who that has the ability would not be ambitious of the honor? If it be honor of too great magnitude for an individual to grafp, let it be divided. Here is enough to adorn many a brow. Oh that all in the higher ranks of life would claim their fhare!"

"If but a few men of fortune and influence had a fpirit equal to their power, what a bleffed country would Britain foon become! The poor would be more happy and lefs burthenfome. The induftrious would live in eafe: the idle and profligate would be reclaimed. Crimes would be prevented inftead of being punifhed. Our prifons in time would fcarce need humane vifitants, but would often (like fome abroad) be almoft empty; at leaft thofe confined in them would be there ufeful to the community, and not dangerous to it when difcharged. Many would go out reformed, and would become good members of fociety. Thus Englifhmen, who vainly boaft of their liberty, would enjoy liberty: would reft in their beds, and travel by day or by night, without fear of being murdered or plundered by their own fpecies. That it is otherwife, is in a great meafure owing to the want of public fpirit in men of rank and power. Would to God that the lofs of ONE Patriot may prove the occafion of raifing up MANY!"

❋❋❋❋❋❋❋❋❋❋❋❋❋❋❋❋❋❋❋❋❋

O D E, &c.

❋❋❋❋❋❋❋❋❋❋❋❋❋❋❋❋❋❋❋❋❋

O D E

INSCRIBED TO

JOHN HOWARD,

L.L.D. F.R.S.

BY WILLIAM HAYLEY, ESQ.

———————"SECOND TO NONE,
IN THE WORKS OF HUMANITY AND BENEVOLENCE."

PHILADELPHIA,

PRINTED FOR JOHN ORMROD, BY WILLIAM W. WOODWARD,
AT FRANKLIN'S HEAD, NO. 41, CHESNUT-STREET.

1794.

O D E, &c.

FAV'RITE of Heaven, and friend of earth!
  Philanthropy, benignant power!
Whofe fons difplay no doubtful worth,
The pageant of the paffing hour!
Teach me to paint, in deathlefs fong,
Some darling from thy filial throng,
Whofe deeds no party-rage infpire,
But fill th' agreeing world with one defire,
To echo his renown, refponfive to my lyre!

  Ah! whither lead'ft thou?—whence that
      figh?
What found of woe my bofom jars?
Why pafs, where Mifery's hollow eye
Glares wildly thro' thofe gloomy bars?
Is Virtue funk in thefe abodes,
Where keen remorfe the heart corrodes;

Where guilt's bafe blood with frenzy boils,
And blafphemy the mournful fcene en broils?—
From this infernal gloom my fhudd'ring foul
    recoils.

    But whence thofe fudden facred beams?
Oppreffion drops his iron rod!
And all the bright'ning dungeon feems
To fpeak the prefence of a God.
Philanthropy's defcending day
Diffufes unexpected ray!
Lovelieft of angels!—at her fide
Her favorite votary ftands;—her Englifh
    pride,
Thro' horror's manfions led by this celeftial
    guide

    Hail! generous HOWARD! tho' thou bear
A name which glory's hand fublime
Has blazon'd oft, with guardian care,
In characters that fear not time;
For thee fhe fondly fpreads her wings;
For thee from Paradife fhe brings,
More verdant than her laurel bough,
Such wreaths of facred palm, as ne'er till now
The fmiling Seraph twin'd around a mortal
    brow.

That Hero's * praife fhall ever bloom,
Who fhielded our infulted coaft;
And launch'd his light'ning to confume
The proud Invader's routed hoft.
Brave perils rais'd his noble name :
But thou deriv'ft thy matchlefs fame
From fcenes, where deadlier danger dwells ;
Where fierce Contagion, with affright, repels
Valor's advent'rous ftep from her malignant
    cells.

Where in the dungeon's loathfome fhade,
The fpeechlefs Captive clanks his chain,
With heartlefs hope to raife that aid
His feeble cries have call'd in vain :
Thine eye his dumb complaint explores;
Thy voice his parting breath reftores ;
Thy cares his ghaftly vifage clear
From Death's chill dew, with many a clotted
    tear,
And to his thankful foul returning life endear.

What precious drug, or ftronger charm,
Thy conftant fortitude infpires
In fcenes, whence, muttering her alarm,

* *Charles Howard, Earl of Nottingham.*

Med'cine*, with felfifh dread, retires?
Nor charm, nor drug, difpel thy fears:
Temperance, thy better guard, appears:
For thee I fee her fondly fill
Her cryftal cup from nature's pureft rill;
Chief nourifher of life! beft antidote of ill!

I fee the hallow'd fhade of HALES†,
Who felt, like thee, for human woe,

* *Muffabat tacito Medecina timore.* Lucretius.

† *Stephen Hales minifter of Teddington: he died at the age of* 84, 1761; *and has been juftly called* " *An* " *ornament to his profeffion, as a clergyman, and to* " *his country, as a philofopher.*" *I had the happinefs of knowing this excellent man, when I was very young; and well remember the warm glow of benevolence which ufed to animate his countenance, in relating the fuccefs of his various projects for the benefit of mankind. I have frequently heard him dwell with great pleafure on the fortunate incident which led him to the difcovery of his ventilator, to which I have alluded.——He had ordered a new floor for one of his rooms; his carpenter not having prepared the work fo foon as he expected, he thought the feafon improper for laying down new boards, when they were brought to his houfe, and gave orders for their being depofited in his barn;—— from their accidental pofition in that place, he caught his firft idea of this ufeful invention.*

And taught the health-diffufing gales
Thro' Horror's murky cells to blow,
As thy protecting angel wait ;
To fave thee from the fnares of fate,
Commiifion'd from the Eternal Throne :
I hear him praife, in wonder's warmeft tone,
The virtues of thy heart, more active than his
   own.

 Thy foul fupplies new funds of health
That fail not, in the trying hour,
Above Arabia's fpicy wealth
And Pharmacy's reviving power.
The tranfports of the generous mind,
Feeling its bounty to mankind,
Infpirit every mortal part ;
And, far more potent than precarious art,
Give radiance to the eye, and vigour to the
   heart.

 Bleft HOWARD ! who like thee can feel
This vital fpring in all its force ?
New ftar of philanthropic zeal ;
Enlight'ning nations in thy courfe !
And fhedding comfort's Heavenly dew
On meagre want's deferted crew !
Friend to the wretch, whom friends difclaim,

Who feels stern justice, in his famish'd frame,
A persecuting fiend beneath an angel's name.

Authority ! unfeeling power,
Whose iron heart can coldly doom
The debtor, drag'd from pleasure's bower,
To sicken in the dungeon's gloom !
O might thy terror-striking call,
Profusion's sons alone enthrall !
But thou canst want with guilt confound :
Thy bonds the man of virtuous toil surround,
Driven by malicious fate within thy dreary
        bound.

How savage are thy stern decrees ?
Thy cruel minister I see
A weak, laborious victim seize,
By worth entitled to be free !
Behold, in the afflicting strife,
The faithful partner of his life,   '
In vain thy ruthless servant court,
To spare her little children's sole support,
Whom this terrific form has frighten'd from
        their sport.

Nor weeps she only from the thought,
Those infants must no longer share
His aid, whose daily labour bought

The pittance of their scanty fare.
The horrors of the loathsome jail
Her inly-bleeding heart assail :
E'en now her fears, from fondness bred,
See the lost partner of her faithful bed
Drop, in that murd'rous scene, his pale, ex-
      piring head.

   Take comfort yet in these keen pains,
Fond mourner ! check thy gushing tears !
The dungeon now no more contains
Those perils which thy fancy fears :
No more contagion's baleful breath
Speaks it the hideous cave of death :
HOWARD has planted safely there ;
Pure minister of light ! his heavenly care
Has purg'd the damp of death from that pol-
      luted air.

   Nature ! on thy maternal breast
For ever be his worth engraved !
Thy bosom only can attest
How many a life his toil has sav'd :
Nor in thy rescued sons alone,
Great parent ! this thy guardian own !
His arm defends a dearer slave ;

Woman, thy darling! 'tis his pride to fave*
From evils, that furpafs the horrors of the
    grave.

Ye fprightly nymphs, by fortune nurft,
Who fport in joy's unclouded air,
Nor fee the diftant ftorms, that burft
In ruin on the humble fair ;
Ye know not to what bitter fmart
A kindred form, a kindred heart,
Is often doom'd, in life's low vale,
Where frantic fears the fimple mind affail,
And fierce afflictions prefs, and friends and
    fortune fail.

* *Mr. Howard has been the happy inftrument of*
preferving female prifoners from an infamous and in-
decent outrage.—It was formerly a cuftom in our
gaols to load their legs and thighs with irons, for the
deteftable purpofe of extorting money from thefe inju-
red fufferers.—This circumftance, unknown to me when
the Ode was written, has tempted me to introduce the
few additional ftanzas, as it is my ardent wifh to ren-
der this tribute to an exalted character as little unwor-
thy as I can of the very extenfive and fublime merit
which it afpires to celebrate.

See yon' fweet ruftic, drown'd in tears!
It is not guilt—'tis mifery's flood,
While dire fufpicion's charge fhe hears
Of fhedding infant, filial blood :
Nature's fond dupe! but not her foe !
That form, that face, the fallhood fhew :—
Yet law exacts her ftern demand ;
She bids the dungeon's grating doors expand,
And the young captive faints beneath the gaol-
or's hand.

Ah, Ruffian! ceafe thy favage aim !
She cannot 'fcape thy harfh controul :
Shall iron load that tender frame,
And enter that too-yielding foul ?—
Unfeeling wretch! of bafeft mind !
To mifery deaf, to beauty blind !
I fee thy victim vainly plead ;
For the worft fiend of hell's malignant breed,
Extortion, grins applaufe, and prompts thy
ruthlefs deed.

With brutal force, and ribbald jeft,
Thy manacles I fee thee fhake ;
Mocking the merciful requeft,
That modefty and juftice make ;
E'en nature's fhriek, with anguifh ftrong,
Fails to fufpend the impious wrong ;

Till Howard's hand, with brave difdain,
Throws far away this execrable chain :
O Nature, fpread his fame thro' all thy ample
    reign !

  His care, exulting Britain found
Here firft difplay'd, not here confin'd!
No fingle tract of earth could bound
The active virtues of his mind.
To all the lands, where'er the tear,
That mourn'd the prifoner's wrong fevere,
Sad Pity's glift'ning cheek impearl'd,
Eager he fteer'd, with every fail unfurl'd,
A friend to every clime! a Patriot of the
    World !

  Ye nations thro' whofe fair domain
Our flying fons of joy have paft,
By pleafure driven with loofen'd rein,
Aftonifh'd that they flew fo faft !
How did the heart-improving fight
Awake your wonder and delight,
When, in her unexampled chace,
Philanthropy outftript keen pleafure's pace,
When with a warmer foul fhe ran a nobler
    race !

Where 'er her generous Briton went,
Princes his supplicants became :
He seem'd the enquiring angel, sent
To scrutinize their secret shame*.
Captivity, where he appeared,
Her languid head with transport rear'd ;
And gazing on her godlike guest,
Like those of old, whom Heaven's pure ser-
         vant blest,
E'en by his shadow seem'd of demons dispossest.

Amaz'd her foreign children cry,
Seeing their patron pass along ;
" O ! who is he, whose daring eye
Can search into our hidden wrong ?
What monarch's Heaven-directed mind,
With royal bounty unconfin'd,
Has tempted Freedom's son to share
These perils ; searching with an angel's care
Each cell of dire disease, each cavern of des-
         pair ?"

* *I am credibly informed that several Princes, or at
least persons in authority, requested Mr. Howard not
to publish a minute account of some prisons, which re-
flected disgrace on their government.*

O

No monarch's word, nor lucre's luſt,
Nor vain ambition's reſtleſs fire,
Nor ample power, that ſacred truſt
His life-diffuſing toils inſpire :
Rous'd by no voice, ſave that whoſe cries
Internal bid the ſoul ariſe
From joys, that only ſeem to bleſs,
From low purſuits, which little minds poſſeſs,
To Nature's nobleſt aim, the ſuccour of Diſ-
    treſs !

Taught by that God, in Mercy's robe,
Who his cæleſtial throne reſigned,
To free the priſon of the globe
From vice, th' oppreſſor of the mind
For thee, of miſery's rights bereft,
For thee, Captivity ! he left
Inviting eaſe, who, in her bower,
Bade him with ſmiles enjoy the golden hour,
While Fortune deck'd his board with pleaſure's
    feſtive flower.

While to thy virtue's utmoſt ſcope
I boldly ſtrive my aim to raiſe
As high as mortal hand may hope
To ſhoot the glittering ſhaft of praiſe ;
Say ! HOWARD, ſay ! what may the Muſe,
Whoſe melting eye thy merit views,

What guerdon may her love defign ?

What may fhe afk for thee, from power Divine,

Above the rich rewards which are already
thine ?

Sweet is the joy when Science flings
Her light on philofophic thought ;
When genius, with keen ardor, fprings
To clafp the lovely truth he fought :
Sweet is the joy, when rapture's fire
Flows from the fpirit of the lyre ;
When Liberty and Virtue roll
Spring-tides of fancy o'er the poet's foul,
That waft his flying bark thro' feas above the
pole.

Sweet the delight, when the gall'd heart
Feels confolation's lenient hand
Bind up the wound from fortune's dart
With friendfhip's life-fupporting band !
And fweeter ftill, and far above
Thefe fainter joys, when pureft love
The foul his willing captive keeps !
When he in blifs the melting fpirit fleeps,
Who drops delicious tears, and wonders that
he weeps !

But not the brighteſt joy, which arts,
In floods of mental light, beſtow ;
Nor what firm friendſhip's zeal imparts,
Bleſt antidote of bittereſt woe !
Nor thoſe that love's ſweet hours diſpenſe,
Can equal the ecſtatic ſenſe,
When, ſwelling to a fond exceſs,
The grateful praiſes of reliev'd diſtreſs,
Re-echoed thro' the heart, the ſoul of bounty
blefs.

Theſe tranſports, in no common ſtate,
Supremely pure, ſublimely ſtrong,
Above the reach of envious fate,
Bleſt HOWARD ! theſe to thee belong :
While years encreaſing o'er thee roll,
Long may this funſhine of the ſoul
New vigor to thy frame convey !
Its radiance thro' thy noon of life diſplay,
And with ſereneſt light adorn thy cloſing day !

And when the power, who joys to ſave,
Proclaims the guilt of earth forgiven ;
And calls the priſoners of the grave
To all the liberty of Heaven ;

In that bright day, whofe wonders blind
The eye of the aftonifh'd mind ;
When life's glad angel fhall refume
His ancient fway, announce to death his doom,
And from exiftence drive that tyrant of the
   tomb :

 In that bleft hour, when Seraphs fing
The triumphs gain'd in human ftrife;
And to their new affociates bring
The wreaths of everlafting life :
May'ft thou, in Glory's hallow'd blaze,
Approach the eternal Fount of Praife,
With thofe who lead the angelic van,
Thofe pure adherents to their Saviour's plan,
Who liv'd but to relieve the Miferies of Man.

SUBSCRIBERS' NAMES.

A

REV. JAMES ABERCROMBIE, A. M. Second Affiftant Minifter of Chrift Church and St. Peter's Philadelphia,

Thomas Armftrong, Efquire,

Mr. —— Argyle,

John Aikin,

Robert Aiken,

A. Argote,

Thomas Allen, 7 copies.

James Akin,

John W. Allen,

Thomas B. Adams,

William Annefley,

B.

Mr. Alexander Brodie,

John Bioren,

Jofeph Bringhurft, junior, 2 copies,

Elijah Brown,

David de Bartholt,

George Barclay,

Thomas Briftoll,

Rev. Jofeph J. G. Bend, Rector of the Epifcopal Church at Baltimore.

Mr. James Butler,

William Brookes,

James Bogert, junior,

Seth Bowen,

Mr. Joseph Boggs, 24 copies,
  Hugh Bigham,

C.

Mr. John Christopher,
  Ephraim Conrad,
James Carson, S. M.
  John Curtis,
  John Church, junior,
  John Claypoole,
  William Clark,
  Charles Crawford,
  Mathew Carey, 6 copies,
  James C. Copper,
  William Cook,
  Henry Cooper.
  Samuel Carver,
  John Cook,
Edward Cutbush, M. D.
Mr. Hugh Cochran,
  C. Campbell,
  James B. Cooper, 10 copies,
Rev. Nicholas Collin, Rector of the Swedish Church
  Philadelphia,
Mr. John Chapman,
  James Cox, Drawing Master,
  Samuel Cochran,
  John Connelly,
  Archibald Crary,
  Andrew Charles, Charleston, S. C.
  Archibald C. Craig.

D

Mr. Thomas Dobson, 50 Copies,
  ————— Dandridge,
  Peter Denham,
  Anthony J. Dugan,
Rev. John Dickens, 10 copies,
Mr. George Duffield, junior,
  James Darrach,
  D. F. Donnant,

r. Silas Dinſmore,
   Michael Duffey,
   Francis Donnelly,
   William T. Donaldſon,
   Edward Dowers,
   John Dowers,
   Benjamin Duffield, M. D.
Mr. Patrick Dickſon,
Rev. Jacob Duché,
Mr. Elias Dawſon,
   Joſhua Dawſon,
Mrs. Margaret Dick,
Mr. John Dorſey,
   William Doughty, two copies.
   Thomas Dungan,

E

Mr. Cadwallader Evans,
   Cadwallader Evans, junior,
   Thomas Enſley,
   Oliver Evans,
   John Ely,
   Eraſtus Edwards.

F

Walter Franklin, Attorney at Law,
Mr. Richard Folwell,
   M. Fennell,
   John Fiſk,
Rev. Thomas Fleeſon,
Mr. Thomas Fitzpatrick,
   Ebenezer Ferguſon,
   Patrick Ferrall,
   Edward Fox,
   John Fiſs,
   Iſaac Fitzrandolph,
   S. Field,
   William Finley,
   Lott Fithian,
   John Fithian,

G

Rev. William Glendinning,
Mr. John Gibfon,
   John Gill,
   David Graham,
   William Gazzam,
   R. Gazzam,
   Francis Grice,
Mifs Mary A. Guerin,
Mr. William P. Gardiner,
   James M'Glathery,
   John M'Garvey,
   John Grant,
   Andrew Graydon,
   W. S. Grayfon,
   D. Grifith,
   John Grifiom,
   William Garrett,
   Frederick Gebler,

H

Rev. Wiliam Hendle, fen. D.D.
Mr. Matthew Hale,
   Edmund Hogan,
   Wilfon Hunt,
   William Hudfon,
   Selby Hickman,
   Duke Harrifon,
   Thomas Hutton,
   James Hardie,
   David Hall, 2 copies.
   George C. Hamilton,
   Jacob Hoffman,
   Jofeph Harding,
   John Hindman,
   Alexander Howard,
   John Hall,
   William Hubbard,
   John Hand,
   William Hogg,

Lieut. David Hale,
Mrs. Elizabeth Hall,
Mr. John H. Hawkins,
　John Heaton,
　James Hamilton,
　Jofeph Hamilton,
　Patrick Hamilton,
　John Henvife,
　Aduan Hunn,
　Jofiah Hewes,
　Ifaac Harris,
　Thomas Harris,
　John Howard,
　Samuel Hyndman.

I & J.

Mr. Richard Johnfon,
　Thomas C. James, M. D.
　Thomas Jones,
　Richard Jolliff,
Mrs. S. James,
Mr. John Jones,
　J. H. Jackfon,
　William James,
　Robert Jones,
　William Innes,
　William Jones,
　Benjamin Johnfon, 100 copies.
　Mordecai Jones,
　Samuel Jones, A. B.
　Nathan Jarvis,
　Jofeph Johnfon,
　Benjamin January.

K.

Mr. James Kennedy, 6 copies.
　David Kimpton
　Emmor Kimber,
　Daniel E. King,
　Michael Kennedy,

Mr. Thomas R. Kennedy,
 John R. Kollock,
Mrs. Catharine Keappock,
Mr. Samuel Keith,
 Ezekiel King,
 J. Kirkbridge,
 Benjamin Kiffman.

L.

Mr. Peter Leo, 2 copies,
 George C. Leacy 2 copies
 Samuel Levis, jun.
 Nathaniel Lee,
 John L. Lewis,
 William Letchworth,
 Mordecai Lewis, — -
 John Lort,
 Caleb Lownes,
 J. Lippincott, ·.
 John Langdon,
 William Leedom,
 William Lewis,
 Michael Lewis,
 Thomas Lawrence.

M.

Rev. Samuel Magaw, D. D. and Rector of St. Paul's
 Church, Philadelphia.
Mr. William Mc'Kinzie,
 James Magoffin,
 James Milnor, Attorney at Law.
 Solomon Marks,
 Mc'Kenzie & Co. 7 copies,
 John Matthews,
Mifs Mc'Clenachan,
Mr. George Middleton,
 John Mc'Kenfie,
 T. Meafe,
 J. M. Ray,
 W. Mathews,
 William Mc'Ilhenney,

Mr. William Meredith,
  Samuel Moore,
  Samuel Minnick,
  Samuel Milner,
  Jacob Mason,
  Christopher Marshall, Minor,
  George Moser,
  John Mc'Kensie,
  Joseph Marsell,
  Maskell Mills,
  Cadwallader Morris,
  John Mc' Masters,
  Timothy Mountford,
  Samuel Miley,

N.

Mr. Heath Norbury,
  Richard North,
  Frederick Newman,
  Thomas Noble,
  Michael Nowise,
  William Norcrofs,

O.

Mr. Jesse Oat,
  J. Oliver.

P.

Rev. Joseph Pilmore, Rector of Christ-Church, New-York.
Mr. William T. Palmer,
  Joseph Pfeiffer, M. D.
  George Pfeiffer, M. D.
  William Prichett,
  Thomas Passmore,
  Isaac Price,
  Benjamin Price,
  Thomas W. Payor, esqr.
  Samuel Passey,
  Norton Pryor jun.
  J. Pouzols,

R

Mr. Nathaniel W. Price, 2 copies,
   Thomas Perry.

R.

Cæfar Rodney, Efq. Attorney at Law,
Mr. John Reynolds,
   Thomas Reynolds,
   Samuel Rhodes,
   John Ruan,
   James Ruan,
Benjamin Rush, M. D. Profeffor of the Inftitutes,
   and of Clinical Medicine,. in the Univerfity of
   Pennfylvania.
Mr. Samuel Richards, jun.
   James Rolph,
   Edward Ruffel,
   Nathaniel Richards,
   Jofeph Reed,
   Robert Rockhill,
   Abraham Roberts,
Meffrs. H. & P. Rice, 25 copies.

S.

Major John Stagg, jun. Chief Clerk in the War
   Office.
Mr. John Sheppard, 10 copies,
   Henry Sweitzer,
   Samuel S. Smith,
   H. G. Shaw,
   W. Spotfwood,
   Samuel Stoops,
   Thomas Stephens, 6 copies,
   J. Strawbridge,
   Thomas Smith,
   John Smilie Adams,
   John Snowden,
   John Shaw,
   James Sawer,
   Charles Shoemaker,
   Samuel Spalding.

Mr. Laurence Sink,
    James Stokes,
    Richard Snowden,
    Robert Salwell,
    Matthew Smith,
Mrs. Surmoln.
Mr. Samuel H. Smith,
    Robert Smith, jun,
    William Snowden,
    Elifha Swinney,
    Jeremiah Seeley,
    John Smith.

T

Rev. Joseph Turner, Rector of the Episcopal Church-
    es at Marcus-Hook and Chester.
Mr. Daniel Trotter,
    Thomas Than,
    John Toplif,
    John Thompson,
    William Taylor,
    J. Ozier Thompson, M. D.
    Anthony Taylor,
    Thomas W. Tallman, Attorney at Law,
    William Thackara sen.
    John Thompson,
    John Townsend,
    James Thackara,
    William Todd,
    Richard Tittermary,
Mrs. Sarah Turner.

V & U.

Mr. R. J. Vanden Broek, Master of Howard Lodge,
    in behalf of said Lodge, 100 copies,
    Peter Van Pelt, Dentist,
    John Vallence,
    Stephen C. Ustick.

W.

Right Rev. William White, D. D. Bifhop of the
  Proteftant Epifcopal Church, Pennfylvania,
Mr. William W. Woodward,
  Jofeph Williams,
  Chriftian Wiltberger, Jeweller,
Mafter John Woodfides, jun.
Mr. Thomas Waterman,
  John Wilfon,
Mifs Eleanor Wilfon,
Mr. Jofeph Wright,
Mifs Kitty Wiftar,
Mr. William Wigglefworth,
  John Wharton, jun.
  Henry L. Waddell,
  John Willis,
  Godfrey Welfer,
  Charles Wheeler, M. D.
  Thomas Wetherill
  Benjamin Wynkoop,
  John Woods
  James Watters,
  Matthew Whitehead,
  Ifaac Warner,
  Francis Wright,
  Thomas Wallen,
  C. R. & G. Webfter, 6 copies,
Rev. Archibald Walker,

Y.

Mr. William Young,
  James Young.

SUBSCRIPTION PAPERS for this work, being in poffeffion of gentlemen refiding in various and diftant parts of the United States; many refpectable names, therefore, cannot be inferted without delaying the publication to an immoderate length of time.

———

The few fucceeding came to hand too late for inferting, in their alphabetical order.———

Robert Gillefpe,
Geo. W. Field,
Peter Fritz,
Jacob Earneft.

R 2

LATELY PUBLISHED,

IN ONE HANDSOME VOLUME, 12mo.

[price 4s. 8d.]

AND FOR SALE BY

JOHN ORMROD,

AT FRANKLIN'S HEAD, No. 41, CHESNUT-STREET,

AN ESSAY ON THE NATURAL

EQUALITY OF MEN,

ON THE RIGHTS THAT RESULT FROM IT, AND ON THE DU-
TIES WHICH IT IMPOSES.

To which a MEDAL was adjudged by the TEYLERIAN
SOCIETY, at *Haarlem*.

CORRECTED AND ENLARGED.

By WILLIAM LAWRENCE BROWN, D. D.

Profeffor of Moral Philofophy, the Law of Nature,
and of Ecclefiaftical Hiftory; and Minifter of
the Englifh Church at Utrecht.

THE grand principle of Equality, if rightly
underftood, is the only bafis, on which
univerfal Juftice, facred Order, and perfect Freedom, can
be firmly built, and permanently fecured. The view of
it exhibited in this Effay, at the fame time that it repref-
fes the infolence of Office, the tyranny of Pride, and the
outrages of Oppreffion; confirms, in the moft forcible
manner, the neceffity of Subordination, and the juft demands of lawful Authority. So far, indeed, from loofen-
ing the bands of Society, that it maintains inviolate, every natural and every civil Diftinction, draws more clofely
every focial tie, unites in one harmonious and juftly
proportioned Syftem, and brings Men together on the even
ground of the inherent Rights of human Nature, of reci-
procal Obligation, and of a common relation to the community.

JOHN ORMROD

HAS LIKEWISE FOR SALE,

AN ELEGANT COLLECTION OF VALUABLE

BOOKS,

AMONG WHICH ARE THE FOLLOWING :

———

BELL's Britifh Poets complete from Chaucer to Churchill ornamented with elegant engravings and Portraits, 109 vols.

Doddridge's Family Expofitor in 6 vols.

Mofheim's Ecclefiaftical Hiftory 6 vols.

Hume's England with Smollet's continuation, 13 vols.

Abbe Raynal's Hiftory of the Eaft and Weft Indies in 8 vols.

Goldfmith's Hiftory of England, 3 vols.

Stackhoufe's Body of Divinity, 3 vols.

The Senator or Parliamentary Chronicle containing a Weekly Regifter of the Proceedings and Debates of the Houfe of Lords and Commons, 7 vols.

Kent's Admirals or Memoirs of Illuftrious Seamen, 5 vols.

Hiftory of Modern Europe with an account of the decline and fall of the Roman Empire, 5 vols.

Memoirs of the Kings of Great-Britain, of the houfe of Brunfwic—Lunenberg. By Belfham, 2 vols.

B O O K S.

Machiavel's works tranflated from the originals, illuftrated with notes and feveral new plans on the Art of war, 4 vols.

Plowden's Britifh Empire.

Cowper's Homer. 2 vols.

Ditto Poems, 2 vols.

Dodfley's Poem's, 6 vols.

Original Poems by feveral hands, 2 vols.

Impartial Hiftory of the French Revolution in 2 vols.

Rabaut's Hiftory of the Revolution in France.

Holwell's Mythological, Etymological, and Hiftorical Dictionary.

Kaime's Sketches of the Hiftory of Man, 4 vols.

Hume's Effays, Moral, Political and Literary, 2 vols.

The Lufiad, an Epic Poem in 2 vols.

Enfield's Hiftory of Philofophy from the earlieft times to the prefent century, 2 vols.

Martin's New Syftem of Philofophy, 3 vols.

Furgufon's Lectures.

Ditto Aftronomy.

Henry's Hiftory of England from the firft invafion of it by the Romans under Julias Cæfar, written on a New plan in 5 vols.

Smith's Wealth of Nations; 2 vols.

Sketches of the Hindoos, 2 vols.

Effay on Happinefs, 2 vols.

Lempriere's Claffical Dictionary.

Stern's Works, 8 vols.

Drydon's Virgil, 4 vols.

Gil Blas, 4 vols.

Spectator, 8 vols.

Herman of Unna, a feries of Adventures, of the Fifteenth Century, written by Profeffor Kramer, in 3 vols.

Thompfon's Works, 4 vols.

Hawkefworth's Voyages, 4 vols.

Seabury's Difcourfes, 2 vols.

New Annual Regifter,

Travels through Cyprus, Syria and Palef-tine, by the Abbe Marite, 2 vols.

Benyowfky's Travels and Memoirs 2 vols.

Adams on Electricity,

Davidfon's Virgil, 2 vols.

Morfe's Geography, 2 vols

Burke on the Sublime,

Mrs. Piozzi Britifh Synonomy, 2 vols.

Annual Regifter,

Perk's Geography,

Gazetteer of the Netherlands,

Bifhop Newton's Works, 6 vols.

Pocket Peerage, &c. &c. &c.